Meow, Monsieur!

Meow, Monsieur!

The French Felines of New Orleans

Translation, Text,
and Illustrations by

Jim Gabour

PELICAN PUBLISHING
NEW ORLEANS 2021

The word "Pelican" and the depiction of a pelican are trademarks of Arcadia Publishing Company Inc. and are registered in the U.S. Patent and Trademark Office.

ISBN: 9781455625550
Ebook ISBN: 9781455625567

Portions of these stories originally appeared in *The Guardian* and on the openDemocracy.net, *Business Week, Wall Street Journal,* and *China Dialogue* websites.

M Grant Morris was a source for two cat observations in the "Gato Negro" chapter. Maps are only approximate locations for stories.

Les avocats français have instructed the author to here legally proclaim that most of the characters in this compilation are based on real cats and somewhat real humans, but for the purpose of the story the characters and some places have been revised, relocated, exaggerated, fabricated, compiled from multiple sources, and in any case are all completely fictitious. *Ils sont tout ça, très certainement.*

Printed in the United States of America

Published by Pelican Publishing
New Orleans, LA
www.pelicanpub.com

For Dad and Minou

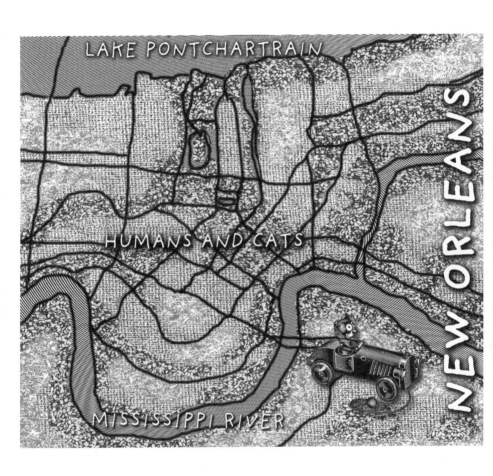

Les Petites Histoires

Preface

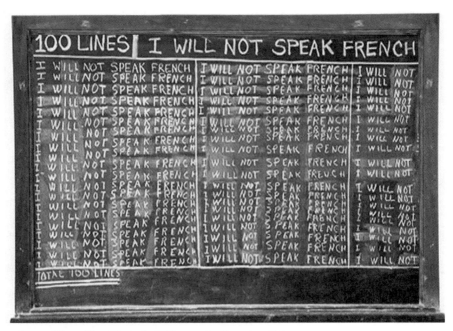

Vermilionville Historic Village, Lafayette, LA

Union troops occupied New Orleans in 1862 and quickly banned the use of French, having decided that the "foreign" language was subversive.

Enlightenment was not to follow quickly. In 1921, a full ban on the use of the French language in schools was again instituted into state law, remaining on the books until 1974.

Dozens of generations of New Orleans cats had only been

addressed *en français* before the human mandate. But as a rule, felines ignore all rules. They are just not interested.

The humans themselves are more pliable to regulation.

Thus, the last US Census indicates that while in Cajun and Creole areas nearly 20% of the people still speak French, less than 1% of the human residents in New Orleans use the language on a daily basis.

The Francophone percentage is much higher among the city's tabbies, tortoiseshells, and Siamese. As observed in these *petites histoires,* among cats the French language is universally recognized — though maybe subconsciously, as felines are also fickle to admit anything — as a direct conduit to the ever-resilient *habitués* of New Orleans.

Meow, Monsieur!

Un être humain, essayant de comprendre le Fred

(A Human Attempting to Understand the Fred)

Upon waking, Fred the cat had a ritual by which he warmed to the world in which he lived. He opened his one (right) eye, licked his right paw and used it to clean any residual sleep sand from the area around his eyelid. He then inevitably executed a mighty stretch with all four paws — and their corresponding sets of mighty, razor-sharp nails — extended. Lastly, he yawned widely, displaying his also fearsome fangs in the process.

"I rule," thought the orange tabby. *"Je décide."*

Fred was angry. Neither of his humans were home. Again. There was nobody with whom he could amuse himself, especially not those other two, older and more complacent cats. Fred was not even sure that he and they were members of the same species. This pair of lesser beasts slept all day and most of the nights, and they were content to solicit food and tactile affection from the humans in their few waking hours.

Not so Fred.

Le chat Fred needed to be the center of attention, always. At all hours. He also needed to be amused, and there was nothing inside the house at all amusing this day. So, to show his displeasure, he peed on the stereo and the front of the fridge.

"That will show the ingrates."

On second thought, he peed on the stereo again, this time focusing on the shiny tuner buttons, for good measure.

He moved regally away from these conquered bits of humanity, complete in his triumph. And as he exited the cat flap that had been fitted into the kitchen portal at the rear of his house, he maintained a sense of pride, backed up, raised his tail, and peed on the exterior of the door too.

"Those two others, they will also have to acknowledge my scent, my superiority," he mused. "If they ever come outside."

"Outside" was a unique concept for this supremely self-assured cat, though he did not realize it. He did not grasp the implications of his own location, living in the lower *Vieux Carré,* one of the few areas of New Orleans' French Quarter that could still sustain full-time local residents. In the twenty-first century, only the last few blocks before Esplanade Avenue, the Quarter's eastern boundary, held onto the remnants of what was once a thriving population of very, very unique individuals. However few, the stalwarts remained.

Fred was one of them.

This morning he made his way around the house, slipping by the tiny window in the back bathroom's WC to crawl under the side kitchen. He emerged in the small yard that ran alongside the traditional single shotgun structure, from the covered porch to the sidewalk fence. He stopped deliberately to sniff each of the various pots that the soft-hearted human female had filled with dirt and weeds, and then had placed in positions eminently suitable for christening.

Fred placed his nose close to the pots' absorbent clay surfaces. Once again the only scent detectable was *eau de le Freddy.* He was gratified. No one else had dared to violate his territory, not even those odd-looking striped creatures with the black masks who came out at night and tried to pilfer the leftovers from his food dish in the darkness.

He thought again how glad he was to be a cat.

"Superior creature," Fred mused, "Superior intellect and looks: it is a good thing."

As he walked toward the front of the side yard and the wrought iron fence that defined its boundaries, he twitched his tail assertively.

"I think I'll do a viewing of the zoo this morning," he thought.

The sidewalk outside the fence was an amusing daily parade of local animal life, plus non-local humans — Fred could tell the difference by their vocal inflections. This was the *Vieux Carré,* the Old Square, after all, New Orleans' quasi-French money-making Temple of Tourism. The visitors sauntered by slowly, individuals and groups, and many of them spoke to him. This day was usual.

A female: "Cute kitty, cute . . . Oh my, what happened to your little eye? Lloyd, did you see this poor cat? Only one eye."

Male: "Shee-yut, Verna, that there is one homely lookin' cat."

Luckily, Fred did not understand human talk, except for words that pertained to his comfort and/or feeding. This was a conscious lack of knowledge. But he could instinctively sense a change in emotional discharge, and here it was again, pitiful beings trying to relate to him. They were not suitable for his notice, though he did consider spraying the metal gate, just to ward off the aura of such creatures. Again, luckily for them, they went on their way before he could motivate himself to shift from his comfortable sitting position, turn about, and aim.

It was a disappointing outing so far for Freddy. His valuable time wasted without a single human-dog pairing passing by his kingdom.

"Dogs. Pitiful."

He loved seeing those creatures, bound by restrictive leashes, with a noose around their necks, strangling them into submission by a human "owner."

"So wonderfully degrading. As it should be," he ventured.

Fred truly enjoyed the opportunity to sit just back from the protective gate, watching the street's walkway and grooming himself, free of all constrictions, while the canines were paraded by, choked into subservience.

While licking under his tail, he again mused: "It is sooooo good to be a cat. *Je suis un roi parmi ces créatures.* Yes, it's good to be the king."

Finally, he detected a jingling in the distance. The sound of deep breathing and multiple footfalls got louder.

"Ah. A prisoner dog. And even better," he thought, "it is one of those two horrid bubble dogs, the pair of them not much bigger than me, who occupy the house that abuts my kingdom out back."

"Wretched little yap-yaps."

Fred was now in fine mettle, lifting his tail and back leg into a perfectly vertical position, and licking his butt slowly and even more casually. He wanted to be in full display mode when the animal and human passed.

And here the pair were, pale thin human male and tiny blonde poodle, its hair sheared into a topiary collage of balloons and bars, its throat encircled by a wide band of multi-colored rhinestones. The small dog, panting and salivating, fixated immediately on the orange cat sitting only inches behind the fence gate.

Fred, of course, refused to look up. His complete disdain for the fierce miniature dog reinforced its frustration, made it furious, even more so because it could not get through the fence and at him.

Sure enough, the dog had not only zeroed in on Fred, but almost jerked its owner onto his knees with a series of colossal pulls on the velvet-lined leash. It pressed its head partially through the fence's bars, barking shrilly, ears hooked on the inside of the gate, its shoulders trapped outside.

"Yap yap-yap yaaap!" the dog screamed piercingly.

Fred had calculated the dog's snout penetration to the millimeter and sat safely licking away within smelling range of the refuse-scented canine breath, not even deigning to look up until he heard the tone of the human's admonition: "Now, Maurice, you are doing it again. Bad doggy! You get back here this instant! I tell you every day, that is just a crippled little kitty, no threat to you. Now stop barking, dammit! Maurice!!! Stop!"

"Yap, yap, yap, yaaappp!!!"

Fred slowly raised his head, mid-lick, blinked his eye slowly, and resumed his ritual. Another slow lick.

The human finally yanked the dog's leash so hard that it momentarily cut off its breathing. There was a sudden pause, then a long ragged wheeze from the poodle. He was being dragged forcefully from the fence, but restarted his barking once he regained breath.

"Yap yap yaaaaaappp!"

His protests, ever fainter, slowly faded away as he was pulled by his master down the block and around the corner.

"A human 'master'! What a concept," thought Fred.

If the dog could have seen the smile on the cat's butt-tilted face it would probably have sacrificed its life to get at him. Fred, on the other hand, was sublimely content. He could go back inside for some lunch now. And maybe a nap.

He was a tad disappointed, though.

"Still no worshippers at the Temple of Freddy. As soon

as I finish this spot of lunch, I think I will go pee on the entrance rug, just inside the front door, so the moment the humans get home they will know my displeasure."

"That is it," he figured, "I need to let them know once again who is in charge. *Je décide.*"

An hour later.

"What's that smell?" asked the male homeowner as soon as he walked inside.

"Oh no, not again . . . Frehhhhhhed . . ."

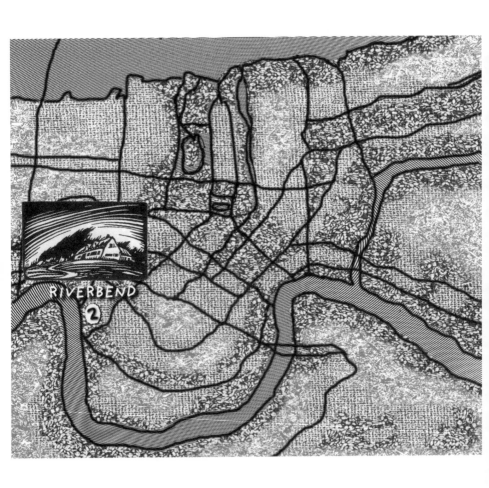

RIVERBEND
②

Un quelque chose
(A *Something*)

Few cats have ever seemed as much at peace with the universe as *Monsieur le Koko*. From the moment the indigo-grey tabby kitten was found sitting in a communal food bowl at the Westbank Mardi Gras Boulevard rescue shelter, to the next-day discovery that he was a boy — he had initially been named after blues singer Koko Taylor on the premise that he was female — he had offered those around him nothing but a constant, warm joy and trust.

When he was presented with a baby sister, a lovely tortoiseshell/calico named Zoë, he welcomed her and helped reinforce her blossoming personality. When he was moved to a new house in the Riverbend/West Carrollton neighborhood Uptown, he adapted and accepted the place as his own.

During the day, if the weather was right, he would sleep in the shady backyard, often flipping onto his back while contentedly dozing, and come in for dinner covered in leaves. When the weather wasn't as perfect, he would curl up with Zoë on the carpet, wondering what was on the menu for dinner, and the two of them would purr loudly, in concert.

Koko was one happy tabby.

Twelve contented years came and went, each night passed with Koko's sleeping head wedged on his human's shoulder, the cat's extended snores resonating as a soft "Kaaay-fuuuurt." His human liked the sound and seemed to sleep better because of it. Koko never moved once he went to sleep at night, his long grey body extended to stretch along the man's right side to below his waist, the cat poised just there until morning.

Koko loved to sleep. *"J'aime dormir,"* he would say every morning as he awoke. He slept soundly, off and on, for a dozen years.

But during the opening month of the thirteenth, his treasured sleep grew troubled. There was a *something,* something new traversing the darkness of each night. Physical and spiritual commotions.

"Sure enough," he decided, "there are spirits of some sort in the house."

Koko was quite positive of that, even though he had never experienced *un esprit.* No matter. It wasn't an issue he worried about to excess. They were simply there, like household smells. Though they could be a nuisance.

He would awake with a start in the middle of the night, knowing there was a disturbance that had brought him up out of his comfortable sleep. It was now just disconnected vibrations and had nothing to do with the bed, the rooms, the humans, his sister, the litter box, or his tuna supply, so he would let it go. But Koko did not like losing his rest, no matter the reason, or how ethereal the source of disorder. Even if it was a phenomenon unreal to humans, it was real enough to him.

There was, however, proof: he found that his ears always tingled when he experienced a *something.* True also, the sound, the vibe, originated not in the bed, not in the room. But from the house.

A *something.*

"Though the humans never seem to notice."

He thought that the perpetrators might possibly be traveling room to room inside the crumbling old structure's thick, badly-insulated walls. There had been mice in there once, but he himself had plotted and executed a plan to flush them out. And catch them. He was known throughout the block as a substantial mouser, and he was not to be trifled with in such matters as hunting intruders.

"If they keep waking me up, I will catch these somethings, too," he thought somberly. "I will catch them."

"Je les attraperai," he asserted.

The third time a *something* noise happened, Koko had been enjoying a most pleasant dream about ingesting a vast number of cans of his favorite, light chunks of fragrant *thon,* tuna packed in water. With a picture of a jumping fish on the outside. The humans called it *too*-nah. But he still pictures it as the savory Gallic *thon.* "Why waste an extra syllable on something so basic?" he often wondered.

But losing the happy fish imagery, he awoke in quite a grumpy state.

"*Mrowf!*" he said aloud, jumping down from the bed, and almost waking his human. It was an impolite term he seldom used, and never, ever without provocation. Luckily, his bed companion had not stirred.

"*Mrowf!*" he said again. He was quite angry, for what was possibly the first time in his life.

"That's it. I have had it with these bad manners! Deprive a cat of his peace and quiet, will they?" he steamed.

He began to slink, in a hunting fashion, through the darkness of the upstairs halls, all his senses alert and ready. He was ready for whatever *something* was out there, so content with his prowess that he had to consciously suppress purring.

Down the hall, down the stairs. Seven steps, landing, turn left. Eight steps, landing, turn left. Three and the ground floor. He knew how many stairs there were and their configuration.

He was on the trail, the mighty tracker, his teeth bared, his claws extended.

Then suddenly: "Mewf."

He jumped two feet skyward and three feet to the left, almost knocking over a lamp.

It was Zoë.

He tried to compose himself, regain his dignity in front of his sister. So he licked his butt.

"Look what I found," Zoë said. "A paper bag."

And there it was, fallen to the kitchen floor.

Koko immediately loosened.

He *loooovvved* paper bags, almost as much as he loved sleeping. He dove inside the large grocery bag and curled up, peering outside. He was very happy, once again.

Zoë stood outside the bag and admired his contented state.

"I saw you stalking, she said. What were you after?"

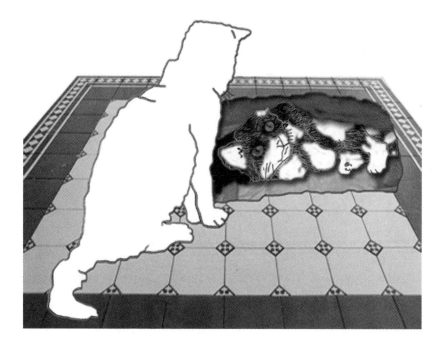

"Oh, nothing," Koko replied, truthfully. "Nothing at all."

"Rien du tout."

It was indeed nothing.

And he never heard a *something* again.

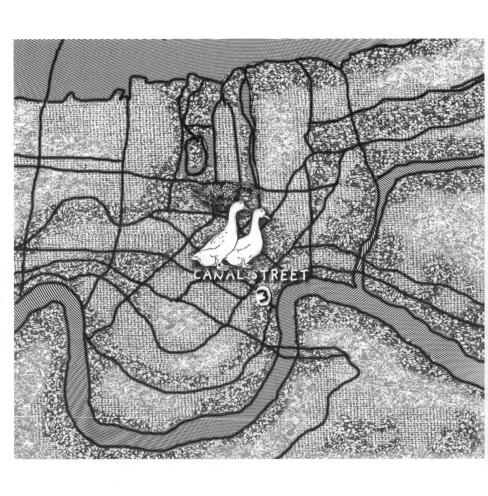

Oh, pour ítre un canard!
(Oh, to Be a Duck!)

Persephone and Paulinho, sister and brother Siamese (with some genetically suspicious dark tail stripes) loved their new digs.

Their human couple, Alice and Dale, finally leased a condo in the newly-emptied *Maison Blanche* department store building. The humans were up against a wall in their acutely-necessary search for suitable housing, with work relocation deadlines approaching for the both of them. Conveniently located in the heart of downtown, on Canal Street bordering the French Quarter. The arrangement was to be a one-year trial, to see if the space and location were suitable to their lives.

It was an interesting idea in any case. Though the department store itself still functioned in the bottom

27

three floors, the hundreds of lawyers, dentists, insurance agents, and full-time investment shysters had been herded from the rest of the building a few months earlier. Now the couple were to be the first inhabitants to occupy a portion of one of the still-unfinished — and non-air-conditioned — top thirteen *étages.* At this point they actually had an entire fan-cooled floor to themselves.

Shortly after paper-signing, the couple found themselves unloading their minimal worldly goods and two cats into a sprawling complex of nearly 5,500 square feet. The seventh-floor suite of rooms they had contracted formerly housed a weekly newspaper's offices and a staff of forty. Now it was just two people and two felines. Even after they had completely unpacked, some rooms remained caverns of emptiness. They simply didn't have enough stuff for all the space. This was not entirely unpleasant, they found.

As of yet, there was no *en suite* bathroom. The closest facility was across from their rooms' north entryway in the center of the block, next to the elevators. Which was some seventy-five feet from the south-facing bedroom, from its high vantage point overlooking the first block of Dauphine and Bourbon streets below. Dale left his bicycle parked by the doorway to the sleeping area, for quicker transport to the remote facilities in the middle of the night. This made for some rather interesting and frenzied nocturnal bike excursions down the complex's pitch-black hallways.

The two cats, meanwhile, loving puzzles and eager to explore every corner available, kept escaping up through the semi-functional industrial doors into service hallways, onto rooftops and down into lightless caverns full of dusty abandoned offices. Their main mission, even though they may have not consciously realized it, was finding cat-routes all the way down. Which meant getting into the inhabited bottom three floors, those still operating as a large bustling *grand magasin,* displaying items for sale from intimate lingerie to restaurant-sized refrigerators.

After more than a half-dozen exploratory sorties, the increasingly adventurous pair reached their goal. The cats found their way down five complex sets of interior fire escape stairs into the department store's prop storage warehouse. There they discovered an enormous area containing everything for the dozens of storefront windows, and the displays for goods in every department and every season.

There were shiny things, and furry things, and noisy things of all shapes and sizes. Some made ominous sounds when disturbed. There was a new experience with every step.

Persephone and Paulinho had found Cat Paradise. And they intended to take some time and enjoy their furry selves.

Their humans were not quite so amused.

Discovering Persephone and Paulinho missing after half an hour of increasingly frantic calls to dinner, the human couple determined that no matter what, they would quickly retrieve their lost family members. They began a thorough search of cat-likely spaces. But the huge, echoing, century-old building was downright . . . well, actually it was *scary*, especially as night fell and the store emptied.

They were also afraid that while they searched, they would trip an alarm or alert a night watchman. So Dale and Alice donned their sneakers, carried flashlights, and acted the part of housebreakers. They had seen the original *Pink Panther* movie recently, and thought they understood cat-burglar stealth.

Again, they were resolved to probe carefully into every available hiding place, until they found their charges. They descended, floor by floor, searching. Then they came upon the infinite maze of the props department.

An hour later the two people were covered in dust, fake Christmas snow, and purple-green-and-gold Mardi Gras glitter. They were beginning to despair ever getting the two Siamese back home.

It was then that they heard the sound.

Maaaaaaa . . . kkk . . .

Maaaa . . . kkk!

Maa . . .

It was the cats. At least it was something cat-like. And whatever it was, it was vocalizing loudly, and strangely. The sound echoed amidst the monumental Santas and buffalo-sized Easter bunnies.

While she would never have guessed the source references of their current communication, Alice had often remarked that the two, Percy especially, often spoke as they explored the condo. Alice had always been fascinated by the way they made mewling sorts of sounds, as the sister and brother conversed with each other about what they were finding or doing. It was almost like they could really talk.

"*Maaaa . . .* your butt is in my face." More politely: *Tes fesses sont dans mon visage."*

The two ever-curious feline delinquents had wiggled into the beak, and slid down the gullet, of a gigantic multi-patterned duck displayed for hunting-season decor. Now they couldn't find their way back up and out of the fowl's steep inner walls. But they weren't unhappy or upset.

Much to the contrary, they were pretending to be ducks,

happily giving up their own versions of ducky quacks. They had seen two smaller versions of the bird a month earlier, splashing about in the large puddle that often accumulated on the flat roof of the adjoining building on Iberville Street. The ducks were also quite vocal.

"*Maaaaaakkkk!*" said Persephone, quite proud of her duck imitation.

Still almost two floors up the stairs, Alice and Dale heard the resonating sounds, and recognized the feline voices, if not what they were saying. They scrambled downwards, pausing every dozen or so steps to restore quiet, cock ears, and try to locate the source of the catcalls.

They entered the lowest prop warehouse floor, and were immediately overwhelmed by the sheer volume of *stuff.* Stuff stacked to the crowns of the fourteen-foot ceilings. Stuff occupying every inch of floor space. Totally irregular bundles of stuff stacked one on top of the other, teetering at the slightest touch. Narrow spaces between the objects, asymmetrical aisles wandering in every direction. No right angles to be found.

"Maaaakkkk!"

There it was again.

Maaaa. . .

Even closer.

"Look there, the giant duck with the ruffled feathers!" cried Alice, pointing anxiously.

"It's moving," said Dale.

Maaaaa . . .

"There!"

Pulling the faux wings back and peering into the literal belly of the beast, the man and woman couldn't help but break into smiles. And, with their tension now gone, fell into loud guffaws. They had never anticipated finding their two pitiful lost cats in such a place. Ironically, devoured by a bird.

Alice and Dale tried their best not to damage the feathered sculpture. They did not want to leave evidence to department store officials that intruders had trespassed into the store. Especially since they, along with the aging and usually snoring night watchman, were the sole nighttime occupants of the building. They would immediately have been the prime suspects. The couple worked carefully and systematically, and after only a few cat hissy-fits, brief breakdowns in feline courtesy, managed to extract the two furballs from their downy amusement park.

The final chapter of the mission consisted of the upright, two-legged creatures scrambling to find their way out of the little-used ill-lit scramble of hallways, and transporting the four-legged prodigals back up the many dark flights of convoluted inner stairs.

Homeward they traveled, finally emerging from the maze of over-blown holiday decor, crystalline merry-go-rounds, smiling bridal-mannequin squads, and neon ball costumes.

They weren't really mad once they were home, the kits fed, and each of them occupied with a glass of wine in hand.

The couple began to speculate aloud, imagining the clever Siamese taking full advantage of their toy-filled surrealist playground. Alice and Dale spoke of the possibilities through a bottle and a half of their hoarded "old vines" — 2013 *Château Fuissé Pouilly-Fuissé Tête de Cru*. In the end, they felt much less frustrated, much less *en colère*. And a tad tipsy.

They had Percy and Paulinho back in the mutual feline/ human living space, and all was well. The undomesticated felines found themselves presented with handfuls of domesticated kitty snacks, as the humans tried hard to bribe their companions into staying home in the future.

Communication of the message, however, was just a tad staged, and unlikely to be absorbed.

"Never again, Percy." Dale wagged his forefinger.

"Promise us, Paulinho." Alice had a pretend-scowl on her face.

Sister and brother looked at each other, dubious about the meaning of these human speech sounds, which in any

case they could barely hear above their own crunching of tasty imitation-tuna-flavored treats.

The ever-considerate human couple should have realized that it was no good trying to reason with Percy and Paulinho, even if they could rise above their munching to understand the nuances of human speech.

Besides, they were both using absolute cat concentration to try and determine better scouting routes to get back to that fat duck.

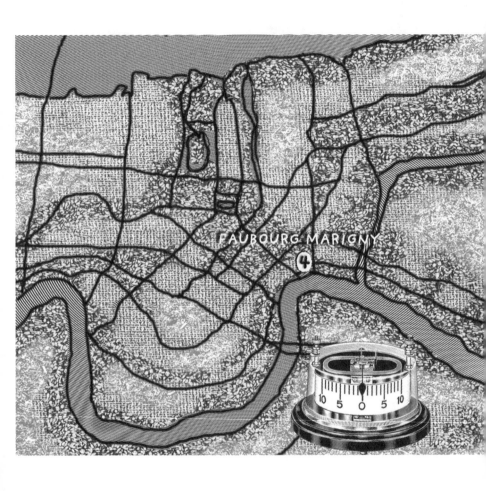

FAUBOURG MARIGNY

Le chat Buddhi ne prend pas l'oiseau
(Buddhi the Cat Does Not Get the Bird)

"What the devil is going on here?!"
Frank, the cognizant human, is addressing footwear.

Buddhi (pronounced "buddy," spelling via human para-religious humor), the sleek black feline, is lying on the bed listening in and observing the other party in the conversation. He really has no idea of what the just-waking man is saying, or even what language he is speaking. He thinks it possibly a dialect of Dog, which he recognizes as another language spoken in loud, short bursts. Each statement always punctuated with an exclamation point, as in *"Bark! Wurf! Bark! Bark!"*

But for the moment at hand, he tries to understand. The Bud astutely notes with a nod of his head the fact that this seemingly self-reliant man has in fact dropped his shoe for the third time in the last minute.

"*Maahh,*" he says, turning to face the balcony door. He stretches, then lies down regally in the classic library-statue lion pose. For the moment the human no longer merits his interest.

"Yes, Buddhi, I know that it is already noon," Frank tells him, though he can plainly see that the day is starting as badly as the night just finished. Stumbling in after midnight and waking the ranking resident cat from his long-in-progress night of snoozing at the foot of the bed. This "adult" behavior did not endear said adult to said cat.

When he first turned on the light, Frank had mumbled something about professional-level, politically-motivated drinking. About the standard of imbibing at the main bar of Mimi's in the Marigny last night, brought on by the latest American political apocalypse.

It continued as a hard night three blocks away, back on Marigny Street itself, even when sleep finally gave some welcome relief in the wee hours before sunup. But Frank was not easily coming awake, and this sluggish progress did not bode well for the remainder of day yet to be faced.

He balances on the rumpled edge of the drastically rumpled bed, mentally scrambled and off-kilter after hours upon hours of tormented, roiled, and broken sleep. He finds that he is having a hard time getting these shoe things onto his feet. The right shoe is forcing him to solve an unexpected puzzle. Cloth laces and leather tongue are somehow tangled in a black, writhing bundle. A simple task is suddenly more difficult than he can manage. He wonders aloud, not for the first time: "How does this stinkin' thing actually *work?*"

Frank bends over to pick up the other shoe, reasoning unconsciously that maybe the left will be easier going than is the right, and . . . bangs his head against an open door of the television cabinet, conveniently lined up to provide concussions, against the room's interior wall.

Buddhi watches and muses. "Coordination is gone. Patience is gone. The human is helpless against the combined onslaughts of an increasingly aggressive universe. Maybe I should eat him."

"Stop that!"

Buddhi turns his head, seemingly amused. After all, the man just yelled at a shoe. Again. Almost slapped it.

Buddy recognized the primary word, one of the few he took the trouble to remember. "Stop what?" thinks the Bud. "Stop not going on his feet? What is the shoe doing, exactly, to make him personally upset? Isn't this the same shoe that went on this same foot so passively, and in such orderly fashion, yesterday?"

Suddenly, loud tapping from behind, coming from outside.

Tap-tap-tap.

"Ignore."

It happens again. Tap-tap-tap.

Tap-tap-*tap*.

"Focus."

Frank turn just in time to see a red bundle of feathers take off from a branch in the tall fig tree beyond the balcony and soar six feet directly toward him, only to hit the glass of the door with his beak. Repeatedly. Hard. And with purpose.

Tap-*tap-tap*.

Buddhi's head is indeed focused. He stares at the very point where the beak touches the glass, every muscle in his body tensed. He sees a meal.

"A meal who looks directly into my eyes for a split second, spins mid-air, and returns to a branch.

"A mere six inches away from his resting spot, a less decoratively feathered female, obviously his mate, sits on another green-leaved limb facing outward toward the yard. She is hunkered down, her back to me, though she seems to look over her shoulder every so often to observe the current interaction."

The male executes another aerial charge, again hitting glass. Three times. Loudly. Aggressively. And again. The female ignores the noise and commotion. Again.

"What in the gee-willy goose-bumps is going on here?!" Frank yells.

Unanswering, the bird returns to perch in the fig tree. Facing the door, the bird looks straight through the human and into his soul. The human gets up and returns the bird's stare. And holds it.

"Rather otherworldly, this concentration," muses Buddhi.

Finally, the man walks to the door and stands close enough to see his breath fog the glass. The bird does not falter, fixated, his eyes aimed directly at Frank.

"Something I can do for you?" the man says as loudly as he can, causing himself further obvious head pain.

That does it. The bird shakes his head, dismisses his audience, and then flies off into the yard. His mate turns to see the source of the last bit of human sound, tilts her head to the side as if she also does not consider the man worth the trouble of a reply, and follows her beau, winging away to the line of citrus trees at the rear of the yard.

Buddhi jumps off the bed and stands at the door, angry that his plans for a winged Happy Meal came to naught because of the human's actions.

Frank's scrambled mind is wondering down historic lanes. "Maybe this is a sign. The Chitimacha tribes native to this area of the Gulf Coast have many legends associated with the local birds — clear indicators of things to come, human activity patterns that can be discerned from avian behavior. Maybe the red bird was telling me something important."

Buddhi remembers that this pair of cardinals has inhabited the patio for the last decade, pretty much year-round.

"Why would they deal with the formidable task of migration when they have access to a dozen fruit trees?"

Buddhi is happy that they stay here. They sing wonderfully. But they are most noticeable visually when the male seems to brighten up a tad, and takes on an ultra-red cardinal tint for mating season. Maybe it is an illusion brought on by the spate of singing after the long cold colorless winter, as cardinals supposedly do not molt, but he does seem brighter when he is horny. Unlike humans.

This violent red versus the female's year-round drab brown. She, with very few hints of the male's majestic spring coloration, is camouflaged while incubating in the nest and being personally fed by her partner. Which is often, as they usually produce three broods of one to three eggs each in a single mating season.

The Bud is pragmatic amidst all the beauty.

"I have heard this pair in my patio warble quite a variety of songs, particularly when the lust is upon them, like now. Maybe soon, I will get to eat one."

Frank thinks differently on the subjects at hand: "Interesting, that after this many years it is still just the two of them here. The youngsters must have headed for greener pastures, and redder males. Cardinals form an unequivocally monogamous society, though quite social. I've seen them chattering along in large groups of birds, even mixing with other species, except when they are hidden away as a couple, spawning and incubating their eggs." He sounds almost rational at this point.

And, of course, then the real facts of the just-completed encounter begin to dawn on the human.

"The cardinal male did not even see me. He was focusing

on his own reflection in the glass — and there perched an audaciously unmoving rival for his woman's affection. Naturally he attacked the tawdry male interloper. Until I showed up and the illusion dissolved."

Buddhi knows this intuitively.

"He just didn't want the fake bird to fool with his girl."

"Here is a naturally-occurring, inwardly-focused alpha

male who makes a huge noise and a physical exhibition of macho behavior while contemplating his own reflection, without regard to anything deeper. Almost human, I would say.

"I, however, am of the ancient lineage of Mouan-gen," thinks Buddhi, "sacred advisor to the legendary doctor of the pharaohs, Shepseskaf-Ankh, who in the fifth millennia BC saved the lives of three successive leaders of Egypt."

"I know our worth to humans."

Frank returns to reality, realizes he hasn't moved for some moments. His hands are clenched, neck tight.

Buddhi looks up at the man from the floor, then bunches his muscles for a graceful jump back onto the bed, where he sniffs the still-tangled shoes. The wise cat no longer cares about Frank's spiritual awakening, and has even forgotten about the loss of an unanticipated meal. He very deliberately drops again into his primary position of physical rest and philosophical contemplation.

Frank, too, lecturing himself vocally, so Buddhi can hear. "I have to stop acting — again as one more self-centered human — that everything in nature revolves around me. It most assuredly does not."

"Ask my cat," he says, gesturing toward his feline companion. "I think even he will not vouch for my worth to the universe at large. Though I am sure Buddhi will indeed testify that, as an opener of cans and bags, I have my uses in his much more deeply-felt and microscopic single world."

That said, with the planet still revolving a bit, Frank has not found a comfortable way to get his feet into shoes.

"Maybe I will just wear flip-flops today."

"There may be no helping this one," thinks Buddhi.

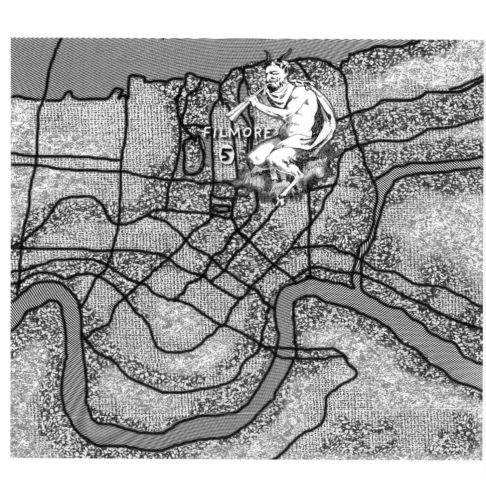

L'Argent affronte la machine du diable
(Silver Confronts the Devil Machine)

"RRRRrrrrr*RRRRRRRR*rrrr."

The roar grew louder and more persistent as it advanced through the house. "RRRRrrrrr*RRRR*rrrr*RRRR.*"

Rhythmic ups and downs in the noise became more evident. And closer.

Silver's ears were already quivering, even though he was upstairs, away from the action. And now his frown deepened. It was one of Those Days. They arrived regularly and unavoidably, as the company of unknown female humans. Every two weeks three or four ladies opened the front door carrying brooms and mops, and always, always pushing the Devil Machine.

The big and normally somnolent grey tabby had no idea

why the aggravating noise inspired such a deep terror in him. It just did. And the nervousness that accompanied that terror stayed with him for days after the Machine had been rolled out of the front door and transported away. An active part of the Machine lingered in the hallways, around the corners, and under the rugs well after the noise had subsided. That was the "devil" part.

Silver could feel it. He had always been sensitive, which was why he had lived so long. He knew when trouble was coming, and got out of the way. He didn't seem to be able to do that with the Devil Machine. The vibrations from its operation hung around the rooms for days, threatening to upend his life. That unsettled feeling often put him off his tuna, giving him yet another reason to resent the Machine's intrusion.

He had no idea why it was brought into the house. It had no easily discernible function. One of the ladies just rolled it around on both floors, seemingly at random. When it hit one of the spaces between rugs, the wooden slats would vibrate even more intensely, and he would always scurry for the cat door to the yard, no matter who or what stood in his way. He had seen and heard the humans laugh as he made his escape, and he had no doubt that this was some sort of concerted kitty torture.

But his own humans were never at home when the Machine arrived and never participated in the noise-making. Never confronted the invaders. Actually, every time, when they arrived back at the house later in the day, they always seemed inordinately pleased, looking about, sniffing the air and touching objects and inspecting tabletops.

There was a repeating drama happening here, Silver was sure. But he couldn't figure it out.

Then, one day the ladies entered as usual, dragging in

their implements including the Machine, but all three of them picked up buckets and cloths, and then went into the food preparation room, where they begin banging about and chattering happily. And . . . they left the wicked device on its own, alone by the front door, its tail partially loose across the floor.

Silver was on the lowest stair landing, discreetly observing the action from his hiding space between the spindles. He saw the Devil Machine abandoned by the humans, standing quietly, making no noise, causing no vibrations. It was obviously asleep.

"Now is the time," thought Silver. "I must not be weak or afraid. I must show this alien beastie that I will not be badgered or bothered by intruders. I will attack!

"Je vais attaquer!"

He dropped into his low hunting profile and began to descend the stairs one step at a time, pausing every two or three to listen for the ladies, for any possible interruption to his plan. And to watch the Machine to see if it remained inert.

Almost to the bottom, and still no movement.

He reached the floor. Front right foot down. Then left. A pause. Back right. Lastly, back left. His tailed swirled about, his attention now focused solely on the Machine. He stayed low to the ground, not allowing his prey a clear sighting of his approach.

And then, there it was. The tail, within reach of his mighty front paws. He pounced, claws extended, ripping the tough skin from the interior bone. He fell on his side so he could use his back claws, too, as he bit and tugged at the tail repeatedly. Skin fell away, revealing the shiny bones underneath. He bit harder, intending a final kill to his tormentor, and felt the bones crunch between his incisors. He pulled harder.

Suddenly, the Devil Machine responded, and began to lurch backward. Silver pulled even harder, sure he was weakening the beast. Then, it lurched to one side, tilted, and fell with a crash against a table. Silver was startled and ran up the stairs again. Finally, stopping at the second floor landing.

There were three simultaneous screams.

"¿Demonios, qué es eso?" came from the kitchen, as the ladies rushed back into the room.

One of them saw the Machine, lying on its back. *"Nada,"* she said, *"Voy a empezar a aspirar esta habitación."* And she picked up the Machine, stuck its tail into a receptacle on the wall, and stepped on a button at its base.

Instantly there was a loud pop, a small flash of fire on

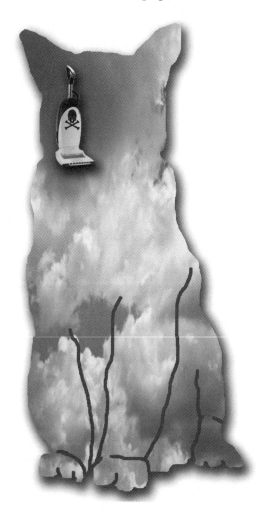

the tail, and a puff of smoke from the wall.

All the lights in the house went out.

"*Mierda,*" the woman said with disgust.

Silver understood that sound. It meant she knew the Devil Machine was dead.

And that he, he alone had killed it.

"*Même le diable ne peut pas vaincre un chat intelligent.*"

It was true: even the devil cannot vanquish a smart cat.

To celebrate, he licked his butt.

ALGIERS POINT

Lire les Russes avec Nigel et Ralph
(Reading the Russians with Nigel and Ralph)

I had, finally, moved in.

An ancient house in Algiers Point on the Westbank of New Orleans had called to me, promising comfort and *tranquillité*. And I had responded, promising a bank my ongoing indentured servitude for a period of thirty years in exchange for a permanent place of residence.

Exhausted and desperate for a change of mental location, I found myself mid-weekend, pawing among the boxes of ancient hardbacks that found their own way out of a great stack of storage boxes, half a dozen toppling onto the living room floor.

Newly adopted Nigel and Ralph were in bliss, celebrating no longer being locked in a bathroom.

I had sequestered them there temporarily until they learned the hygienic function of a litter box. Released, they claimed the cardboard-shipping-box Mount Everest as their private plaything, and the stairs their constant challenge. Two furry demons flashed through the house at an unrestrained speed, knocking over whatever dared stand in their paths, and hissing wildly at unresponsive objects they could not dominate.

The two kittens had appeared in the front yard just inside the torn cyclone fence a week earlier, ill-fed and obviously looking for sanctuary. I caved on my first look at them.

But in spite of being "free" pets, they were very expensive. Long-haired and evenly pewter-colored Ralph occasionally got too excited and went into one of his wheezing fits — a result of an infantile pulmonary infection, said the doc-on-the-clock vet. For this, Ralph got multiple antibiotic shots. Plus, I gave him the vet's twice-daily prescription to clear it up, which had some small effect. But his malady only slowed the fun action momentarily, and as soon as he rattled out the last deep cough that signaled the end of his spell, he was instantly back on the run with his brother.

"Mackerel" (swirl-sided fur) grey tabby Nigel had a slightly askew front paw, which gave him less refined propulsion skills, but he could romp just fine. Neither kitten's infirmity put the slightest dent in their capacity for happy mayhem.

I was glad for the companionship, since the house was totally quiet on this night. Except for the cat circus, all I could hear were the low moans of foghorns on the river three blocks away. Always protesting too much company, since moving into what could easily become my upstate family's private New Orleans hotel, I have been reticent about invitations to visit at this early stage of my own habitation.

But I am feeling awkwardly abandoned this particular evening.

I should have done something useful, but I couldn't. I wanted the luxury of reading, something I had neither the time nor energy to do for what seemed months. If I could

take a few moments to enjoy reading, I could consider yet another transitional portion of this life adventure successful. That is to say, survived.

First, I had to actually find a book. Some stomach queasiness was involved in the removal of thick, badly wrinkled layers of packing tape, seeing as how their texture instantly evoked an ancient flaking zombie sunburn. But that nasty tape was all that gave shape and structural integrity to the otherwise flimsy cardboard of the packing boxes. After a ten-minute struggle with a serrated bread knife, I finally managed to open the first heavy cube, only to discover its contents to be a portion of my full set of *Collected Classics of World Literature.*

I sighed, remembering this as what it was: a long-ago, high-school graduation gift of matched, beautifully bound, gilded, and parchment-leaved volumes that were now covered in the dust of at least two decades of blatant disuse. They had been dragged between multiple dorm rooms and then into a long succession of rental apartments through college and continuing through post-grad, real-life re-education, as part of my debt to Western civilization in general and familial ties in specific. My *grande-tante* Marthe, to be very, very specific.

I have acquired a house of my own, settling down for the long and final rush into rooted senility, and I still haven't raised the courage to put all these irrelevant volumes in a garage sale.

There, on the pecan wood floors of my home, rested the unpacked *Classics*. Forty-five volumes collectively brooded at the possibility of being removed. They intimidated me just as much as the self-possessed, blue-haired matron who had given them to me. In the end, they knew full well that they would somehow escape the trip to a sidewalk table.

What if my ninety-year-old expatriate *grande-tante française* Marthe ever came to visit and all forty-five volumes weren't prominently displayed? Could I ever sell them to a stranger? The woman would sense the retailing of her gift all the way back in her home *Américaine,* where she had settled in Grosse Tête, Louisiana. She'd get on her aluminum walker, scrape along one hundred and twelve miles of interstate highway and appear at my door, looking for her books. Just the searching look on her face would be enough to generate palpable guilt.

"What then of your own personal search for *l'âme de l'homme,* the soul of man?" she would lecture. "Have you now decided to abandon the timeless realm of human literature for transient, cheap comic books and sordid *pornographie?* Eh? Will you just disappear without a trace, without having made a mark in this abysmal place? *Qu'en est-il de votre vie, mon enfant?* What about your *life?*"

She spoke like that, even after she had moved into "assisted living" in a very *Américaine* hospital annex. Yet my *grande-tante's* universe was ordered, and no one had best try and upset it. The *Classics* had moved with me yet again. And again.

I was too tired to search any further. I needed to get

settled in a tub and read. So it was to be one of my great-aunt's *Classics*. I started pulling book after book out of the box. Nothing but tomes of *Nineteenth Century Masters* and a resoundingly deep moan.

After extracting the first layers, I remembered why long ago I stopped reading authors of that vast era. The books were palpable embodiments of depression. I kept digging, opening covers. There wasn't much to be found that didn't start right in at "Chapter One" seriously pondering fate, describing a plague, or weeping outright over an untimely death.

In spite of that, I still found myself carrying the chill of the Russian steppes to the hot solace of my tub on a Saturday night. At least they were "exotic."

Hunkered down in the ancient tub of a very basic, undecorated but monumentally renovated structure — full of humming new appliances, gleaming copper pipes, and whistling air conditioning ducts — a child's muse returned. In these novels, for the intelligentsia, the sensitive, the enlightened, and the artists, there was always that threat of an incurable, prolonged death from something called *consumption*.

Yes, yes, yes. I know now what they were describing was an actual physical ailment. Probably tuberculosis. But still, the worst disease the literati of the day could imagine was *consumption*.

And it remained so. "Especially for me," I thought, sliding deeper into the bubbles. "I am lost to consumption."

"This is very, very depressing."

Just then, as I gazed straight up at the ceiling in a profound, metaphysical, quasi-Cyrillic sulk, my nose just above the level of the water, there to my left appeared two bright furry faces, with four even brighter eyes.

Nigel and Ralph, residents for only this very short while, had already been able to sense my state of mind and come to counsel me. The fact that I was lying so deeply in that wet stuff made them even more concerned for my well-being. I held up my hand to their faces and they began

actively nibbling on my fingertips, holding onto them with their tiny paws.

That was all it took. The spell was broken. I sat up and gave a damp smooch to each of their heads. Ralph took a swipe at my cheek, and fell off the side of the tub. He tried to immediately act like nothing had happened and bit Nigel's tail. Nigel said, *"Fooooonffff,"* and swatted at his brother, simultaneously losing his balance and splashing into the tub with me.

He instantly levitated upward and out, with only the tips of his paws getting wet. It was an amazing, gravity-defying performance. I had witnessed the phenomenon of Cat Magnetism. Feline scientists could readily confirm that water does indeed hold an opposite electron charge from cats, and repels them with a force. Nigel flew from my tub with a minimum of moisture contact. He licked the remainder of the offensive liquid from between his deeply striped toes.

Laughter felt pretty damned good. I almost choked. I guffawed. I heard the sound of my alternating coughs and *hees* echoing through the house and knew that spirits were on the rise, in more ways than one.

Consumption. Material acquisition was evil. It must be. Look how miserable I was just a few minutes ago, dwelling again on how I am smothered in possessions. But these two guys volunteered. If me acquiring Ralph and Nigel, or them me, made me a consumer, I didn't give a damn about it. I was going to open a can of tuna and make all three of us happy.

The *Classics* went back in the box, and their prospects for travel were strong.

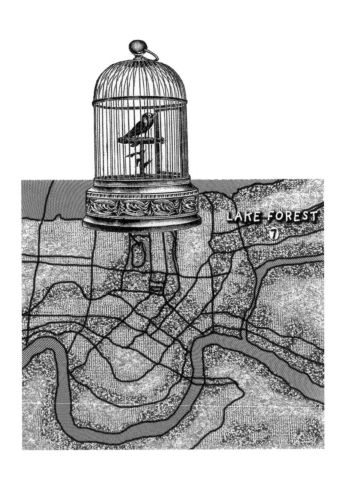

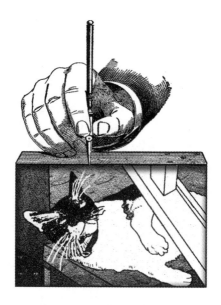

Daisy se demande d'ou elle vient
(Daisy Wonders Where She Comes From)

The sickly mother passed away shortly after childbirth, unable to nurse. And so, despite the veterinary assistants' best efforts, only one kitten from the litter survived the second week. It was a female, destined by coloration to become a calico. She was a tiny, fragile being, her mottled skin almost transparent in some places.

Her eyes weren't even open yet when Angela Vo saw her at the SPCA the day after her university graduation. Angela had decided that, empowered by her new master's degree in geography, she could and would nurture the mewling little being into health. She deserved a reward. So Angela signed the papers agreeing to bring the kitten back for her shots and other health-related procedures within six months, paid the adoption fee, received two more weeks' worth of instructions on nurturing, and then walked her new charge gently through the Deep South sunshine, into her small American-made automobile.

She spoke to the kitten, kissed its tiny head, and braced the cloth-swaddled form in the palm of one hand. Then, with the other, she began to maneuver her vehicle through the long journey from the Westbank animal shelter, across the massive Crescent City Connection bridge, toward her home in New Orleans East.

It was all she could do to keep her eyes on traffic and drive, as she found herself desperate to visually soak up more of those first moments. *"Tu es si belle.* You are so beautiful," she whispered in a pink ear, bringing the kitten close to her face, pressing it against her cheek.

Angela lived in a small white frame house with green shutters and a white picket fence, located immediately next door to her parents, whose own house sat in the heart of the sprawling Vietnamese neighborhood clustered around Chef Menteur Highway and the community's Catholic church. They were Vietnamese immigrants who had come to New Orleans from what many still called French Indochina, and whose prolific bread bakeries and ongoing chain of Roman Catholic baptisms testified to many generations of French influence.

As a graduation present, the doting mother and father had bought the empty lot next to theirs, and commissioned her father's first cousin's construction company to build a "totally American home" for their daughter, celebrating the first child in the family to obtain an advanced degree. Even though they had no idea whatsoever how anyone could make a decent living with a master's degree in geography.

Hers was also the first generation with unaccented, evenly-Americanized English speech patterns. All shades of her Vietnamese, and most of her French, had been banished, in wave after wave of stateside schools. Though she still fell into the comfort of French every so often, as her grandmother had. She was what her parents had been hoping for all along, since the family escaped a doomed Saigon in spring of 1975, and ultimately settled in New Orleans. Her father, once a highly-decorated major in the

Army of the Republic of Vietnam, had worked thirty years as a Gulf fishing boat skipper to support his family in its new environment.

The Vos wanted Angela to be happy, and even more, they wanted her to stay close to home. She was their only child. If she got married, she could raise their grandchildren right there, next door, only steps from their kitchen. That way they could supervise family development, nurture the next generation, and protect her from her husband, whomever that might be. They thought that now that she had completed her strenuous years of study and had a secure future and home, she might finally even meet somebody, gather some friends — or that husband.

But at her moment of integration into the real world, the only individual outside of family who could claim a personal acquaintance with Angela was a kitten who weighed less than a pound. Who looked up at her with unseeing, pink-lidded eyes and seemed to smile. "Like opening a brightly-colored flower," thought Angela Vo. *"Comme une marguerite."*

"Or like a *hoa cúc*. Maybe even a *người lạ lùng*."

"No," she happily concluded, "she's like a *Daisy*."

The weeks and months passed quickly, Daisy put on weight, walked upright, opened her eyes, looked around, and began springing off the walls of the small house in complete kitten glee. She slept every night next to Angela, purring the both of them to sleep. And during the day, when the young woman had begun teaching at a neighborhood science high school, Daisy would lay on the big red chair in the house's front room. Where she dutifully waited for her much-beloved mother to return.

Finally, just over six months into their life together, Angela felt her kitten was strong enough to get inoculations, undergo a med exam, and face a certain "other procedure." She had researched the matter carefully, and found a pair of veterinarian sisters practicing near Esplanade Avenue in the Bayou St. John neighborhood, both of whom were rated highly for their skills and of equal strength in their empathy with clients, two- and four-legged alike.

Angela booked an appointment, bought a carrying case, and drove crosstown to sit in a waiting room with her rapidly-growing kitten. Daisy didn't get upset when she was placed inside the case. She remained content. The box was just an extension of their home, especially since the little room was being carried by her mom, who still lovingly called her *"Marguerite"* from time to time. She purred.

While they were waiting for their appointment, a gentleman with another carrying case came to sit down next to them. The door of the case, facing Daisy's own container, revealed a large grey tomcat, a little worn and battle-scarred, but seemingly friendly enough. He began speaking to Daisy almost as soon as he and his human were settled.

"I'm Duke," he said, in sounds the cats both understood, "I totally *own* two blocks of Mid-City, off Orleans Avenue."

"Daisy," she replied, in kind. The two owners smiled at each other, hearing the *meows* and *frrrrrts* going between their two cats, and struck up a conversation of their own.

"Maximilian Legrande, but they call me Max," said Max.

"Angela Vo, but they call me *Miss* Angela," said Angela.

"I bet they do," said Max with admiration.

Down in Max's lap, the Duke continued, disregarding the human speech going on above the boxes: "Gladta meetcha, ma'am. Where ya come from?"

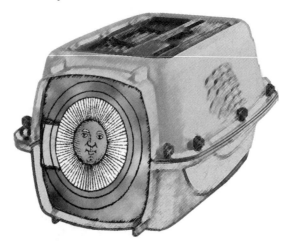

She thought about that. "Where **do** I come from?" She thought again. And thought some more. She got it.

"From my mom's side at night, and the big red chair during the day. That's where I come from," said Daisy confidently.

"Ah, hon," rolled the big tom's voice, "but dere's a big wide wurl out dere — Tremé, Gert Town, Black Pearl, Carrollton, West End — I been ta all dose places. Dere's a lotta stuff out dere for dose of us of da fee-line persuasion."

At that moment Angela Vo's name was called.

About two weeks later and no longer sore, Daisy was still thinking about what Duke said, wondering what else was out there.

When Angela came home that afternoon, Daisy meowed at the front door, walked past her without another sound, and went outside on her own. Angela watched in surprise. Daisy had never done this before. So Angela walked with her cat into the front yard, onto the sidewalk, and watched with interest as Daisy very intently looked up and then down the street. The *fee-line* was absorbing the outside *wurl.*

Angela tried to imitate her cat's actions, and donned a serious face while wondering about the reason for the observation.

But then from below: "That's it."

The young now-worldly-oriented cat looked up at Angela. Daisy meowed with feeling, directly to her mom.

Angela nodded, and they went back inside.

The young human began to prepare a cat meal.

"I may have some news later, *Marguerite,*" she said directly to her feline charge. "Max called me today."

Daisy was lying down in the big red chair, waiting for time to go to bed. She could feel positive energy being transmitted from her mom.

"OK, good. Got it."

"I've seen it now," thought Daisy, proudly.

"I'm from here."

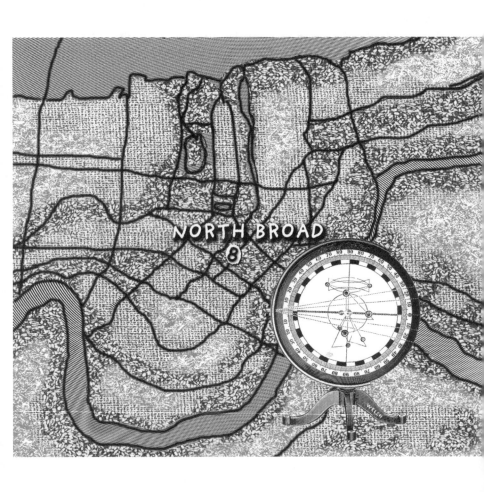

NORTH BROAD

Le chat noir trouve Le Chat Noir
(The Black Cat Finds The Black Cat)

Unlike French, Spanish continued to blossom in New Orleans.

Feliz Corazon's grandfather Solitario moved to New Orleans and founded the business that would become *La Botánica del Gato Negro* in November of 1956, shortly before Fidel Castro and Che Guevara landed in Cuba's Oriente Province aboard the yacht *El Burro Enojado*.

"I got out before the whole *confusión* started," he always said. "We had nothing when we came here, not even a *gato negro* of our own."

It took over a half-century before a black cat would take up residence at The Black Cat. By then what had started as a small *tienda cubana,* serving plate lunches and sandwiches and lottery tickets, had succeeded in the

63

unlikely transformation of its business into the premiere *Botánica* of New Orleans, the big box store of hoodoo.

But the Cat became itself very, very gradually.

Over the progress of many years, Solitario had passed the store to his son and then to his grandson, and Feliz Corazon had become well-known as most powerful among the *brujos* and their African and Creole counterparts, the *traiteurs* or folk doctors, of New Orleans. The family controlled much of the mojo hardware of both the city's east and west banks, of the Mississippi River, and had become a force among the followers of both voodoo and Santería.

Feliz had followed his *abuelo* in migrating to New Orleans from Miami because his magic was considered too dark for the Florida crowd. The people there gave him *su respeto,* their respect, but were too frightened of his reputation for harboring dark magic to actually bring him their custom. Even the parish priests in Little Havana had refused to hear his confession.

So, in 1981, he moved into a musty bedroom in his grandfather's house in New Orleans, a town well-known as an old world village where the blackest of arts seemed an everyday matter, and where the *La Botánica del Gato Negro* now sat prosperously on a main crosstown street corner.

In later years, some of the store's most-popular, low-cost stock was actually made up of castoff secondhand holy cards of Catholic saints. The current Corazon buyer acquired the yellowing pieces of printed cardboard at a discount from a religious clearing house in Galveston, Texas, and used them to form the foundations of the Corazons' next-generation cottage industry. Feliz's seven-year-old son, Andrés, was president of *Las Cartas de la Buena Fortuna LLC.* His job was darkening beatific Anglo faces each night after he did his math homework. *El Presidentito Andrés* was paid three cents a tan, bringing the per-card Corazon investment to five cents. The Gato sold them *"en descuento,"* "discounted" to $2.99 apiece.

With their heightened color, the religious figures received different names, each a remnant of the century-old half-remembered religions of freed enslaved people.

Almost everyone who came into the *Gato* was still a devout practicing Catholic. But images of the powerful black cat were everywhere, in multiple posters and statuary in the shop. The duality of beliefs never seemed to worry, or even occur, to them. Divine origins also did not trouble *El Corazon's* cash register.

When the skinny black feline showed up at the store's back door, meowing for a handout, Feliz did not hesitate for in instant. "Our *gato* has arrived," he announced, carrying a chicken leg to his new business compatriot. And in keeping with that primal connection, his name was announced as simply "Gato." But with a reverence for his status.

It took only a month before Feliz recognized that the small animal was special. He already believed that any creature, including cats, could be in two places at one time. *"Es verdad,"*

was his pronouncement. It was a settled fact of religion, he told everyone who walked into the store, and began relating the story as a matter of course in the *Botánica.*

As a first simple example, he would tell how his Gato would meow to be let out and then stop in the doorway, refusing to move, believing himself to be both in and out of the shop at the same time. He was still safe inside with his benefactor and yet he wandered the sidewalk banquette, looking for adventure.

"Aw, man, c'mon," would often be the reaction of his listeners. "Don't sound like much to me."

"I know," Feliz would say in response, shaking his head. He had been holding back, as part of his process of logical storytelling. "There's more, and better to be told. It's *el espejo.* The mirror. Gato loves to sit in the downstairs bathroom sink, facing the mirror, seeing his world in its reflection. When I come into the room and speak to him, Gato talks to me in the mirror, not turning around. That cat thinks that both he and me exist in both places. *Un milagro!* And who is to say he is wrong?"

Feliz was an educated man in such matters. He was an expert, certified with an online degree in paranormal terminology. It was his business. "Of course, cats have the ability to bi-locate. They are multidimensional." His customers liked the words. They were reassured with the complexity. Feliz was a doctor to them, after all.

He cited new developments on something called the "Schrödinger cat paradox," which holds implications for quantum mechanics. *"¡Implicaciones profundas!"* he crowed. This paradox, he explained slowly to his patients, actually did state that a cat could be in two places at once.

"To start with," he continued, "this truly creepy, *horripilante,* imagined experiment that some Nobel Prize *européen* scientist named Erwin Schrödinger thought up in the '30s and '40s. Goofy name, *Shrow-dinger,* but this *coco* collaborated with *Albert friggin' Einstein."*

He let Einstein's identity sink in.

"The Schrödinger *hombre* came up with the idea to leave a cat alone in a box with some sort of *cosa loca* that would

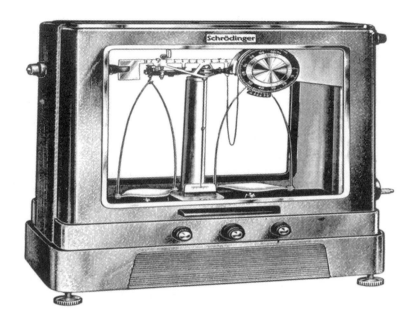

allow it to kill itself — *piénsalo, amigo,* think about that craziness. This made the cat both alive and dead at the same time. So until the box was opened, and somebody found a dead or a live cat, the cat was actually in two places at once."

Why a cat and not a dog, or mouse or monkey?

"No se," Feliz always admitted, "I do not know. But the *científico* chose a cat."

Bi-locating cats are an actual scientific phenomenon, he promised everyone who would listen. And they did.

Hello, *Gato.*

The cat had coincidentally appeared at *La Botánica* in the aftermath of a New Orleans hurricane, quite literally blown to the doorstep from someplace else. Why the black cat chose a place called The Black Cat was part of Feliz's paradox. Another part was his magic.

Was he *still* in two places?

Not if it had to do with boxes, Mr. Schrödinger. *Gato* definitely didn't like boxes. Not for pooping, not for transportation to the vet, definitely not for metaphysical co-existence. Maybe he had caught the gist of the human storytelling.

Feliz said that Gato was the most mysterious, unapproachable, and absolute mystic of cats. As befitted his station as *Patron de Gato Negro*. Gato seemed to honestly want to belong to the *Botánica* family, but he didn't want any member of the family actually touching him. To assert his independence, when a new customer arrived, he would walk out the double doors and onto the street, sometimes disappearing, then re-appearing, and then disappearing again, for many days at a time. But always in the end, returning and looking like he had been through an ordeal.

Feliz and the staff came to love and admire Gato as something of a feline shaman, because when in-house he would sit on the counter and inspect the customers, one at a time. He would look through anyone who approached the cash register, through that human's outer defensive covering, into their soul.

That person inevitably would feel the piercing inspection. And often felt better. Remarked on it. And told their neighbors.

"Gato crawls right into you when he looks at you with those soulful eyes. And yet, there he is in front of you. *Un milagro!* A miracle!" Feliz would exclaim.

And so, Gato became a big draw for customers at the *Botánica*. People often called to see if *el gato negro* was in residence before they would come to shop.

In the real world, though, Gato was aging rapidly and developed a non-functioning liver. He stayed behind the counter more, and even let Feliz hold him as he got sicker and sicker. The Corazon family fought long and hard to keep him alive, even giving him daily saline injections and expensive drugs prescribed by a holistic vet.

Then came a morning when Gato finally looked Feliz in the eye and said goodbye. During the day he slipped out the front of the shop once again and disappeared a final time. Feliz lit a dozen of his most expensive candles and prayed for a month that Gato had bi-located, gotten well, and would return.

But he never did.

LOWER GARDEN
DISTRICT

9

Butch et le coffre très grand, très bien verrouillé
(Butch and the Very Big, Very Locked Box)

Contrary to his macho name, Butch was a delicately constructed tiny, pure white kitten, with one blue and one gold eye set into an immediately appealing face. His fur was silky and of moderate length and he had a very long pink tongue that he would completely extend when drinking water. His humans considered it a singularly adorable trait, among many. And they valued his young self all the more.

He could charm anyone, human or cat, with just a tilt of his head and a blink of his pale lashes. He was not "butch." He was just Butch.

Butch was also, in keeping with a unanimously-held, universally-feline trait, incredibly curious. For such a small creature, he harbored an inordinately large and

71

active portion of this curiosity thing. And even though he could not actually describe or even recognize "curiosity," he was also quite smart. Human smart, even.

He and his humans had moved into the old house in the Lower Garden District, not far from the river, and immediately started a process that he would in a cat identify as "pissing in all the corners." They were making the house theirs, freeing it from many generations of previous owners. Butch could empathize with this.

"Cleaning the catbox," he thought, "totally understandable."

So when his humans struggled to pull the dusty black trunk down from the attic, he was mildly interested. When they began hitting the trunk's many locks with hammers and still were unable to open it, he began to watch with considerable interest. When they bloodied their paws badly, and then yelled at the trunk for a long period of time, he was downright titillated.

The trunk said nothing, and still refused to open. It was no longer very dusty. It had lived in the house a long time, through any number of owners, and not much bothered it. Or even tried to.

The man and woman began to pour liquids from a bottle into small stemmed glasses, and muttered to each other while glancing back at the black box. They had not planned on a large unidentified presence in their new house, and were not happy, Butch surmised.

He began to speculate.

"It is a large thing," he thought, "meant to contain other things. And from the way the humans had to scoot it down the ladder and along the floor, it must be heavy and have something even heavier inside.

"What could that be? And why would it have been placed inside something that cannot be opened? Maybe it is a really large fish." Butch hypothesized.

"Humans seal fish in cans, and the fish lasts for many years until the cans are opened with a very special tool.

"And then I get to eat the fish.

"So maybe this is actually a very, very large fish, in this

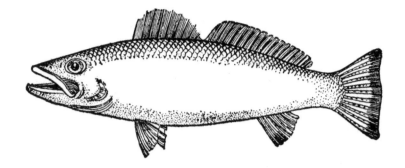

very large can, and they simply do not have the correct tool. Not yet.

"What would the tool be? I am getting hungry just thinking about this problem.

"Fish would be good."

The man had left the room while Butch was thinking, and now returned with a large device with a jagged and pointy metal stick at the end.

When the man pressed a notch in the device, it made a loud whirring noise, and the pointy part moved back and forth quickly. It seemed quite agitated. The man smiled and moved toward the trunk. He aimed the device at the locks and pressed forward.

"Ah, so he has found the can opener. I was right! Fish!" Butch thought happily.

Butch was ecstatic, vindicated in his reasoning, and his hunger was vastly amplified.

The man extended his arm. The device touched the trunk, and instantly scraping noises and bright hot sparks exploded all through the room. Butch crawled beneath a large chair and watched from its fringe by the floor, hypnotized by the battle at hand. Human against can. More dust, more sparks, and loud noises from the human, as he pressed the can ever harder with his opening device.

Then, just as the mêlée reached a raging frenzy, an incredibly loud *"Ding!"* echoed through the house. The pointy thing shattered. The can opener coughed once, and sputtered to a stop. It was smoking. The man threw the device to the floor and made more muttering sounds, even more aggressive this time.

The woman came from behind the door where she had hidden from the commotion and joined in. She was visibly shaken by the can's refusal to open for her partner.

"Damn!" she said, really loudly. So loudly that even the man jumped.

Butch jumped, too. He did not know what a "damn" was, but he was sure it was not pleasant.

An idea came to him. "Maybe it's a brush! An extra heavy brush. I like brushes."

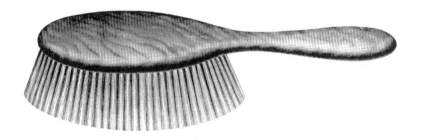

But then he realized that a brush just wasn't heavy enough. And it would rattle around in the trunk.

"Too bad, I would have liked to be brushed."

He brought his feline imagination to bear on the problem.

"Or . . . it could be one of those large things I see roll onto the flat stone beside the house. Humans can fit inside and roll around. They are heavy."

"That might fit in the trunk, if the people were small enough.

"Je ne sais pas grand chose de ce genre de choses," he realized.

And it was true. He just didn't know much about those roll-around things. Especially size and weight.

Butch watched as the man walked back over to the very large locked box and kicked it. The woman had again gone through the door, and when she re-entered the room, she

had a variety of small objects in her hand, which resembled some of the shapes that were fastened to the outside of the box. Shapes that the man had hit with the hammer. She began to try and match up small pieces of metal with larger objects on the box.

This means of attack, Butch could not quite suss out. He tilted his head and looked again at the woman and the box, thinking a new angle might make the operation more understandable.

But it did not. To the cat, the objects were not only inscrutable, but upon sniffing at them from a distance, inedible. Just as well. The woman grew frustrated again quickly, shook her head, made the *"damn"* sound, and threw all the objects to the floor. There were a lot of them.

Butch thought they made interesting noises as they bounced to a stop. Tinkling and banging and such.

The house slowly quieted. The red liquid in a second large glass container was now gone, the stemmed glasses now empty, and the human couple was much calmer, even sleepy.

They had seemingly given up their assault on the box. For the moment. Butch heard "Let's go to bed," and though he did not understand the words, the slurring sleepiness of the vocalized sounds convinced him the day was over.

He stared at the box for a long time after they left, trying to wrap his cat-wise mind around the reality and concept of the very large, very locked box.

"There has to be a reason it refuses to be opened, I wonder if it could contain something even larger than a car.

"What if it contains *us?*"

The very thought made Butch wag his tail to and fro in quick jerks.

"Yes, what if *we* are enclosed by the box, rather than it being on the floor here in our world?"

He walked around on top of the trunk, reaching over the side from time to time to touch the locks and hinges.

"This will never open, he decided. Not here, not ever. We all might as well be inside, protected by the unbreakable box."

And, having thought that, he began to develop a headache.

"That is enough of this silly human thinking."

Promptly forgetting the day, he ran into the humans' bedroom, hopped up on the vast bed, and snuggled into the rumpled covers between their feet.

The humans snored.

Butch purred mightily.

The next morning when the two humans and the one cat got out of bed, they went about their daily wake-up activities without incident. They washed and he groomed, and they all three ate breakfasts of various sorts, and then the two humans went off to work in the rolling thing, quite happily.

There was no mention or sign of a box, no evidence of a struggle to open it. The new house was clean and in order.

It was a beautiful day inside and out, and without conflict.

Except that, around noon, Butch looked through the kitchen window and saw a very strange, very light-footed, very skinny black cat walking warily about, capturing all the backyard scents.

Oddly, it was rather hard to see. As soon as Butch looked directly at the intruder, it seemed to shift elsewhere.

Like it was in two places at once.

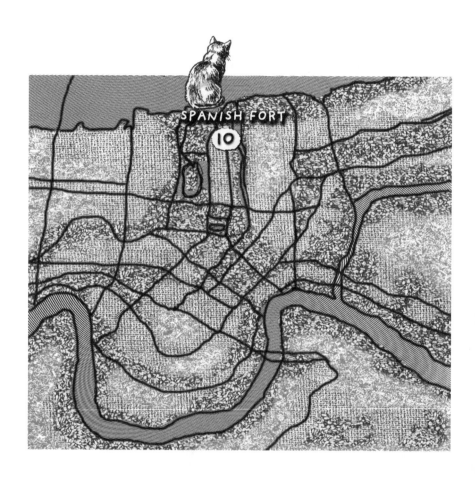

SPANISH FORT

10

Minou, le Vieux Pet, et la Vie Sauvage
(The Pussycat, the Old Fart, and the Wild Life)

In spite of his French name, "Minou" translates into something much more than a generic "Pussycat."

He earns his keep by guarding the fig and pecan trees out back of his house in the Spanish Fort neighborhood on Bayou St. John, near its outlet into Lake Pontchartrain. He recognizes the fruit and nuts as food sources for his much loved and much aged human, *le Vieux Pet*. Food is important, no matter the species, disposition, or age.

He acts casual, lying about and grooming himself nonchalantly under the pecan tree. At least, until the squirrels who steal the human's hard-won food source, and who have at first shied away at his arrival, boldly return to the ground to gather up the windfall nuts.

Minou then eats the squirrels.

For fig protection, he lies passively by the fig tree until the cardinals and mockingbirds who peck holes in the prized figs lose their fear and actually start to dive-bomb him, pecking him on the head as they swoop down, making raucous victory-over-cats birdcalls.

He usually allows them three pecks.

Minou then eats the birds.

He does not require canned food after consuming small mammals or birds. He usually signifies this by bringing whatever remains of the deceased vertebrate to the foot of *le Vieux Pet's* chair to show him the prize. He proudly displays his kill, to show that at least *he* is still young and independent of food sources, whereas the Pet requires flesh-food caught and killed by a third party. Food acquired by an exchange of paper to an oversized human "supermarket" thing, explained by his human as a vendor quite remote from the act of hunting.

The process had been transmitted to him with signs, show-and-tell, and props, by the (yes, repeat for emphasis) sometimes grumpy, always loving, and increasingly aging Pet.

However much he cares about the man himself, the tabby considers this manner of food-gathering to be dishonest.

His own behavior he considers both moral and practical, though people often find it to be a rather discomfiting display. Visitors to the house have expressed serious distress when Minou brings a prize into the living room for praise. This has occasionally occurred during human dining events, which seem to amplify the emotion brought on by the exhibition of rather bedraggled animal remains.

Some of these amateur feline psychologists blamed this catch-display on maternal training. Not in this case. Minou had little, if any, knowledge of a mother before wandering into his current home as a very, very young kitten.

What then? Why does this soft-hearted, gentle creature persist in what would be considered feral activity?

The Pet had investigated. It turns out that there are many non-behaviorist theories on this phenomenon. Some are more scientific, even chemical, asserting that cats, unlike dogs, cannot digest plants. And that they need *taurine* to live, a chemical only found in raw meat.

So even though Minou gets the metal cylinders of tuna, *taurine du thon,* he still finds it part of his domestic responsibility, and his secret to long life, to get outside, exercise, and gather his own. He is not an evil creature. He just needs his *taurine,* yes, yes.

And he has an even stronger instinct to provide for his home. During Louisiana's protracted hurricane seasons, and the weeklong passages of such storms, Minou will wait until a lull in the winds to rush outside, acquire prey, and bring it back to the house, proudly displaying his catch at the front door.

"I can provide," he advertises.

The comestible of choice is usually his second-favorite bird, however, because only mockingbirds are arrogant enough to dare the simultaneous wrath of both weather and Minou.

Some people put bells and bibs on their cats to make them less efficient hunters, or have their claws surgically removed, or take to making them overfed and fat, or simply

just lock the cats inside. This is all very ironic, since it was cats' abilities to hunt and therefore keep mice and other animals out of human food sources that first attracted men to felines.

The "Old Fart," by virtue of the depth of knowledge acquired in his 103 years on this planet, gives all due deference to Minou. He knows that his current longevity is in no small part due to the attention and feline care bestowed upon him by his own "pet."

"Pet." Those English-speaking humans hearing Minou being tagged as a generic "pet," and approving, will never know that Minou calls his human the same thing in French; *"pet,"* meaning "fart," and even *"vieux pet,"* which, of course, translates as "old fart," Again, Minou loves his Old Fart. He doesn't care that most people will never know what the word means in French. But for him, it is a term of affection, one the Old Fart even occasionally calls himself.

And, of course, Minou considers loving *le Vieux Pet* as a primary part of his responsibility for ownership of the house, which he does indeed own, as cats will do. Though he seems to have misplaced the notarized papers. Maybe in his box? *"Le papier n'est pas bon pour beaucoup d'autre,"* he thinks. Paper not good for much else.

Up on an otherwise quiet Bayou St. John.

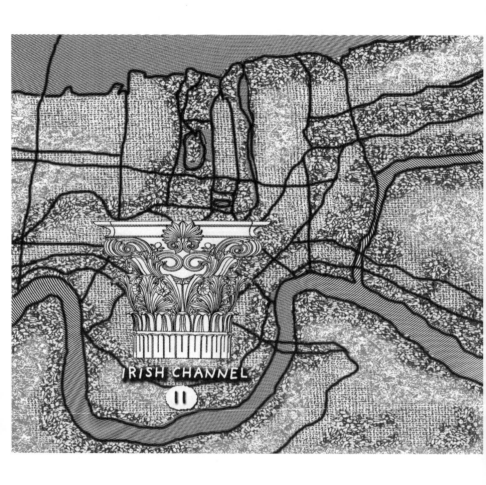

IRISH CHANNEL

À la recherche de la sainte Gertrude, patronne des chats
(Searching for Saint Gertrude, Patron Saint of Cats)

In a small hidden-away public space in New Orleans' Irish Channel, there resides a shrine to one St. Gertrude. None of the neighbors will own up to knowing anything about the origin of the concrete Corinthian column with the "holy card" of St. Gertrude set under clear epoxy on its top surface. Or acknowledge maintenance of the three-foot square of greenery, with its occasional bouquets of street flowers. "Not into voodoo!" and "I ain't even Catholic!" are the normal rejoinders.

But even the most non-religious neighbors comfortably proclaim a fondness for the quaint site, if no knowledge of the woman it honors.

It seems that Gertrude of Nivelles (whose birth is variously attributed to every year between 621 and 628 A.D., but who was most definitely and unanimously confirmed dead, once and for all, in 659 A.D.) was a human now known as the patron saint of gardeners, travelers in search of lodging, widows, recently deceased people, the sick, the poor, and the mentally ill. People call upon Gertrude for protection from mice and rats, fever, insanity, and mental illness. Foremost, for the last two centuries, Gertrude has come to be known as the patron saint of cats.

Despite all this patronage, she was never actually awarded formal canonization. Though, over a thousand years after her birth, in 1677, Pope Clement XII saw fit to give her a universal feast day, March 17. Which she unfortunately shares with the vastly more well-known Irish St. Patrick. Who was himself also never canonized by the church. It is possible that March 17 is a catch-all date dedicated to patron saints who aren't actually saints.

Gertrude was born in Landen, a town located on the southernmost edge of Flemish Brabant next to the French-speaking south of Belgium. So though she spoke Flemish, it is not surprising that one of the few sayings supposedly attributed to her is in French. *"Pourquoi ces chats malodorants me suivent-ils tous?"* she is touted as having said. Even then the venerated nun was being followed by cats with malodorous habits.

When Clement XII ascended the throne of St. Peter in 1730, he was also not known to be a fancier of felines, though he seemed to think that a long-dead nun named Gertrude, burdened with many post-mortality responsibilities, deserved some recognition.

Cats or no cats.

There is no liturgical record of any cats being polled, or even consulted, to see if they desired or approved of having a human patron saint.

Some theological scholars have long since speculated that had cats been given the choice, they would have preferred patronage from one of their own.

With a Feast Day of March 17, of course.

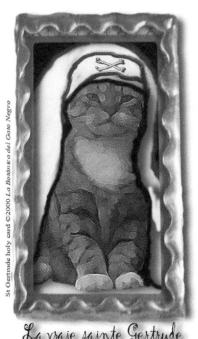

La vraie sainte Gertrude

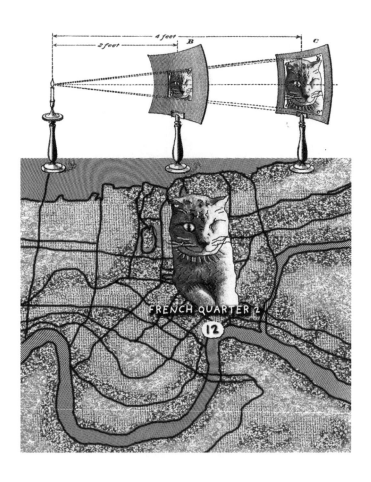

Mystères du Tigrou
(Mysteries of the Tigger)

He was deserted by his mother at birth and survived by his wits as a literal infant. He begged for food from seedier neighborhood hangers-on, those scarcely better off than he. He scavenged for meals through rotting garbage in restaurant dumpsters, running between shadows on the precarious New Orleans lakefront. He occasionally trapped a fish, which had strayed into the shallows or found a recently dead crab washed up on the shore.

He slept in abandoned cubbyholes hidden in the maze of small, damp caves that crisscrossed beneath the jagged concrete of Lake Pontchartrain water breaks. Riprap, they called it.

He managed his own life for well over a decade, with help from no one.

Then, as he was trying to cross a street, once again scrabbling for food, he was hit and critically injured by a car. The vehicle rolled over him, and did not stop to help.

Neighbors saw his injury, ran to the accident site and tried to find him. But, like sole survivalists are wont to do, he had instantly gone to ground to try and recover on his own. Other than recent blood stains, there was not even a sign of him to be found when that help first arrived. When by pure chance he was discovered weeks later by a rescuer, he was on the verge of death, had lost one eye, all his teeth, and the use of a leg. His tongue was split down the middle. Untreated, his bones had fused incorrectly.

He was in constant pain, and tried as best he could to communicate that distress. His volunteer doctor ordered him to be taken for rehabilitation to a wooded inland farm in Mississippi, a place that catered to such lost souls. He had really just been settling in there when in 2005 Hurricane Katrina came ashore south of the place, inundating the coastline with a thirty-foot storm surge. Trees and dwellings were considerably thinned.

He survived again, and even began to thrive, together with others of his ilk and age for the first time. By that December he had recovered enough to be offered for adoption on the internet, his story accompanied by a picture of his tortured, though admirable, face.

An adoptive family was not considered a likely result. Even the rescue agency itself admitted that a permanently injured, toothless, and half-blind thirteen-year-old was a long-shot for adoption.

They were out there though. And they had experience with one-eyed cats. Serious experience.

The infamous *Le Fred* had made a major error a year earlier, when he had attempted to attack both his neighboring poodles at once, in their own yard. It had been a valiant, though doomed battle.

Hearing of Fred's gallant demise, nearby dog-owning residents of the French Quarter had breathed a deep sigh of relief, sorry to hear of any mortality but knowing that the tormentor of all things canine had now moved to a higher realm. Tourists traveled on rented bikes through the streets of the Lower Quarter not even suspecting that they had missed one of its greatest, and most haughty, attractions. *Le Fred* ruled no more.

Through an improbable chain of events starting with his adoption picture on the internet, and the fact that the couple had lost a one-eyed orange tabby, the limping three-and-a-half-legged fellow came to live with the late Fred's humans.

"Tigger" they called him. He was already tagged as "Tiger" when adopted, but the old boy was much too loving and non-aggressive to be called that, and so his name was softened with another "g." He weighed twelve pounds, 5.4 kilos, when he first arrived in New Orleans' French Quarter.

Much of Fred's painstakingly applied scent, once permeating the residence, had already faded by then.

The Tigger gained weight and then a feeling of safety, and he thrived on a steady diet and much petting. But he never gained a voice. For many years Tigger had known that the secret of survival was maintaining a low profile and being absolutely quiet. Completely still. So he did not speak, ever, even now that he was safe and loved.

And he was actually loved, for the first time. Tigger knew this to be true.

Suddenly, after months of stability and care, those measures of happiness were declining hourly. Something bad had entered his system, and his breathing became more labored by the moment. At first the doctors thought it was a harsh uprising of asthma, and then, a possible heart attack, sending some sort of embolism from lungs to heart. It was the Memorial holiday weekend, his regular vet was not available, and the emergency clinic where he first was treated had confined him overnight to an oxygen tent.

In the process of diagnosing his condition and evaluating his ongoing status, they performed a number of scientific and medical procedures, including taking a life-size X-ray.

They looked inside his thick orange fur and discovered even more of his history. There was a bullet lodged in his side. It had been there some time and had scarred over. Two of his spinal vertebrae were crushed in what were probably the jaws of a large dog. He had many, many other healed wounds.

All this violence was attached to the touchingly affectionate creature that had slept purring with his head and front paws on his humans' hips for all those past months. They had never realized before the X-ray just how far he had come, how much he had endured. Yet, here was a creature still able to blot out past horror and simply offer himself as a loving presence in other's lives.

That nervous Sunday morning, while they waited for word about Tigger's imminent transfer to a different, much better-equipped, and vastly more expensive critical-care facility, the couple began thinking that this old tabby and his now-discovered contents had made them begin separating faces and lives, and stories. Maybe this was his function on earth, offering himself as a reminder for compassion on a personal scale.

Though at the time they feared that both they and the cat owed that Bush fellow, still the "W" president then, a debt of sorts. That Saturday, before taking Tigger to the first emergency room, the mail arrived with an "economic stimulus payment" — a check from the federal government made out to the male for $600. Then, just hours later at the ritzy veterinary critical care hospital, he was required to put down a deposit on the Tig's bill: the hospital's finance person demanded they pay $600 before she would admit him for care. Exactly $600. Which, confounding George W. Bush's economically subterranean policies, they gave to the hospital and did not spend at Walmart.

No matter, George. All of us eventually die anyway. Only the worth of the story remains.

Tigger would tell them that they all matter, if he could. He himself matters, here in this hard place where creatures live and die at the whim of their fellows. Where the self-aware are ruled by the caprice of the planet on which they are allowed to momentarily exist. To occasionally use the litter box. Then to not exist.

They spoke to the doctor later that day. The tabby was awake and purring in his oxygen tent. They went into the treatment room to read him the Sunday paper's comics section.

Tigger liked the way his humans pointed out the brightly-printed shapes. He even recognized some of the two-dimensional depictions.

"There are speaking cats in those pages, felines who are in control of their lives," he thought.

Whatever brought him release, was the couple's motivating force. He was not well, you know, and to heal he needed brief respites from the pain of reality. As do we all.

Two humans and a cat went home. They continued to enjoy the fantasy lives of cartoon characters together every Sunday. If a cat could be said to laugh, it is certain that Tigger did.

And at 11:31 a.m., exactly one week after he was released from the hospital, Tigger said, out loud: *"Mahr!"*

A cause for celebration, that.

 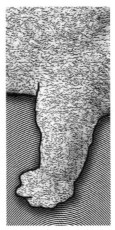 

Lenny croit que Pahoo est determine a dominer le monde felin

(Lenny Believes Pahoo Is Intent on Feline World Domination)

LENNY

I know my cat. He sits right here in front of me at the moment, as attentive as ever, and with a knowing look in his eyes. Though he, of course, cannot understand a word. Or doesn't care too, unless it involves his own well-being.

Nevertheless, Pahoo is a brilliant, self-assured, mottled-silver-and-black feline, whose name I derived (with his permission) from the Golden Age of TV, 1958-59. It first appeared on a show called *Yancy Derringer*. The suave, French-accented voice of the ladies' man of the title derived from late nineteenth-century New Orleans, and though outwardly a riverboat gambler, he was really an undercover crime fighter.

That alone should have been enough to insure a network hit, in my humble opinion.

But in spite of that grand premise, era, and location, the show lasted only two years on the boob tube.

The "Pahoo" monicker came from the inscrutable Indian who always guarded Yancy's back. The character Pahoo-Ka-Ta-Wah carried only a knife, concealed under the cape behind his right shoulder. His Native American name was explained on the show to mean "Wolf Who Walks on Water."

Interestingly enough, the suspiciously-dark-tanned actor who portrayed Pahoo was credited as being himself named "X Brands" in the non-acting world. That was Pahoo, alright. "X" stands for unknown in algebra, after all.

I called him by his newly minted name when he first arrived as an adopted stray kitten, that transaction via a new girlfriend. The girlfriend left after two months. The cat stayed.

He looked right at me and blinked slowly. The "X" factor had sealed the deal.

He is Pahoo.

PAHOO

Lenny is not a bad human, just a very insecure one. He believes he is not in control. And, of course, he is probably right.

This is why he talks to himself, and lectures me. In this convoluted and incomprehensible human language.

It is a good thing I am sensitive to a wide range of communication.

LENNY

Pahoo's influence on my life is possibly why I became so interested in a recently published book: *Infectious Madness: The Surprising Science of How We 'Catch' Mental Illness,* by Harriet A. Washington. It seems they found a parasite that cats transmit to humans called *Toxoplasma gondii,* which "appears to make those who harbor it more sexually aggressive."

You mean that wild, totally unwarranted attraction to the roller-derby barmaid that I briefly endured at age 30 was Pahoo's fault?

Omg, yes!

PAHOO

I can tell from his agitation, and the scent of testosterone, that he is speaking of that hormonal surge he had some years ago over a female.

She was taller than him. Way taller. Procreation would have been difficult, in many ways.

LENNY

Maybe Ted Nugent was right, way back in 1977. Remember "Cat Scratch Fever"? You should. Like most tunes of the era, it was about sexual attraction. VH1 named it the "32nd best hard rock tune of all time."

A lifetime achievement, being 32nd best, Ted.

And now it's scientifically proven, though not the same as that mentioned above.

Nugent's reference is to yet a different cat-borne, though coincidentally parallel, malady.

The Big Guy of kitty fever is this *Toxoplasma* highlighted in Washington's tome. Even the Mayo Clinic warned recently: "the parasite forms cysts that can affect almost any part of the body — often your brain and muscles, including the heart."

Supposedly the infections occur when humans come in direct contact with cat poop, i.e. changing the litter box.

PAHOO

He wrinkled and held his nose, and then pointed at me, indicating a smell attached to my own cat self. He must be talking about "The Box" again. Lenny gets minimal exposure to this domestic item, I promise you.

I've actually been a yard pooper for almost a year and he hasn't even noticed. Or changed the dirt in the box.

LENNY

I found another treasure trove, an article from *Proceedings of the Royal Society, Biology* 2006, that makes even bigger assumptions about a parasitic microbe found in cats: "in a survey of different countries, Lafferty found that people living in those with higher rates of *T. gondii* infection scored higher on average for neuroticism, defined as an emotional or mental disorder characterized by high levels of anxiety, insecurity or depression."

Whoa, this does it, Pahoo! I am blaming everything on you. I am calling the Prez this afternoon. We have found a new scapegoat!

PAHOO

Laughing now. At my expense, I think.

Meeeoooooowww, boy.

Lenny is again hoping I will take his burden, whatever that is.

LENNY

The Royal Society also says the parasite "is thought to have different, and often opposite effects in men versus women, but both genders appear to develop a form of neuroticism called 'guilt proneness'."

Oh no. Guilt too?

Get **outta** here! Now I *am* wearing gloves and a mask to change the litter!

These scientists are saying I am getting sexually aggressive, groveling for more money and material possessions, all the while feeling even more guilty about those failings. And that now, instead of just attributing such actions solely to being an American male of a certain age, I can say that my cat did it?

That Pahoo is responsible?

Yes, yes indeed. I really *loooovvvve* my kitty.

PAHOO

You know, he's not really such a bad guy.

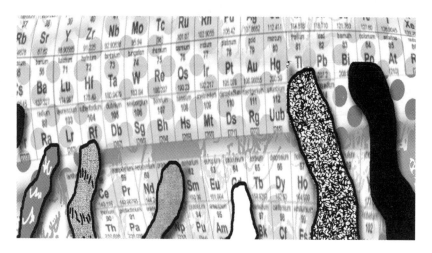

ALGIERS POINT 2

Deux chats chantants
(Two Cats a-Singing)

August. Good grief. Another year slipped by.

It's been so damned long. The house renovation has been "done" for some time, the place is fit for habitation, and I am no longer its slave. I've now been holed up with various work projects for the past six months, to pay that relentlessly recurring house note, and I haven't had a free afternoon here in New Orleans for what seems years. No Happy Hours at home. What's the use of living in one of the decadent centers of the world when you spend days kneeling at the *prie-dieu* of work?

Doing penance without getting to enjoy the sin is simply wrong.

This day seems to magnify the fact that once again I'm here alone in the house. With two dozing cats. On an extremely hot afternoon. Doing nothing except electron-filtering the universe though a plastic and glass workstation connected to a billion other workstations around the globe. None of whom are enjoying Happy Hours. This is to be my fate for the next couple of decades, unless I do something drastic.

It's so quiet that I can hear Ralph and Nigel snoring. Literally. They get so deeply and contentedly into their unconscious Inner Cat that they sing in their sleep. From the far end of the living room couch comes Nigel's blissful warble: "Kay-pheeewwwwww." Answered almost immediately by Ralph's resonant: "Kay-*pheeewwwwww-onck-onk-onk!*" Ralph often punctuates his snoring with loud sounds, as he dreams of chasing purple-throated chameleons and large swallowtail butterflies in the patio. The two cats' simultaneous performance is an ongoing duo, destined to last until evening meal time.

Feline meal times now rule my life. It is solely my fault that it has come to this. Since the rest of the time I work or eat or sleep in a rather unstructured daze, the only two events that *must* happen in each 24-hour cycle are a morning meal for two at six, and an evening meal for two at six. Ralph and Nigel stand on my chest and screech until I get up in the morning, and stand on my keyboard and screech in the evening until I once again head for the kitchen as ordered.

Of course, there is dry food out all day and night. But the feeding ritual is something that somehow reinforces the cycles of their lives. And enslaves mine. Sometimes to the point of claustrophobia.

But they will be fed. And I have no other recourse than to feed them. It also gives my day, week, and month structure. When the stack of tiny cans drops below a certain level, another seven days has passed and I must scurry to the store. It is my bane.

Though, of course, I do enjoy their enthusiasm and their show of gratitude once I fulfill their feeding ritual. They both purr in unison as they eat. The two brothers in cathood do many things in unison.

Including sleeping. Which they do all day at the moment.

Because it is summer in New Orleans. And except for the two felines, who from June until October worship daily at the altar of air-conditioning — often sleeping on the floor vents — there's no one else stirring about in the house except me, and that does not promise Kitty Fun. None of that to be had in me these days. So for them, sleeping is the more enjoyable recourse. Better than going outside.

Of course, no sensible creature wants to be walking about in New Orleans in malaise-filled August. If you've a weak spot, the last month of summer here will bring it to the fore. But my own personal angst cycle recurs far more regularly than one month a year in recent times, it seems. I can't blame it completely on the heat, this making myself neurotic while everyone else easily rides the spiritual and thermal tides with no problem whatsoever. At least I think they do. I have no real experience in the matter.

Even reading my *grande-tante's* multivolume survey of world literature would offer no respite.

Today I am determined to get out of the ongoing negative pattern.

I decide that to break my self-imposed, consummately-boring rhythm, I need *go to a Happy Hour.* Namely, a very specific Happy Hour that I have seen advertised on flyers posted on telephone poles near the ferry landing, with specials that run through the afternoon. Conveniently, it is located on the river road, deep in the heart of Algiers Point, very near my house.

Four blocks, and a light-year of soul-confusion, away from where I sit within the embrace of the house's AC, in front of this blue-lit computer monitor.

I must go.

I wave goodbye to the two sleeping feline princes. They do not break their circadian rhythms for a microsecond.

"Kay-*pheeewwwwww.*"

". . . *onk!*"

Endlessly and effortlessly repeated.

I put on my straw summer hat — which I haven't worn in about two years — and walk. Only to quickly discover that initiating this hypothetical self-help project may have been a major physical error. It is incredibly, *incredibly* hot. Incredibly is not temperature-descriptive enough. Maybe if I use it again: *incredibly.* Hot.

I turn onto the shadeless street just below the concrete river levee wall. The sun is bearing straight down, the heat inescapable. Everything street side is painted with an overpowering slather from the meteorological palette — bleached sun white.

I traverse the blocks, one after another, sweating. On the positive side, I notice as I approach the bar that there are people outside its doors. There is an abundance of lively talking and gesturing. There are paper flyers advertising afternoon bar food. This, at a place where in my prior experience the doors used to only open, grudgingly, at five p.m. Great. It has been a while.

At this very moment I resolve to also open earlier.

I push the screen door aside to find the room inside extremely electric. At four p.m. There are dozens of people enjoying themselves in conversation. And at least one very loud, borderline too-old-to-be-doing-that, woman is seemingly howling at the universe in general.

Hipsters, *aging* hipsters is the term that immediately comes to mind. Khaki with leather accoutrement. My wardrobe is consummately out of tune.

Tattoos, torn jeans, and unrestrained dogs are the order of the day. I do remember hearing from my AC maintenance man that this is to be expected as the norm in the Point, so I accept the environment immediately.

The bartender wears a sleeveless shirt, displaying his muscled arms with some bravado. The left is tattooed completely black from shoulder to wrist. There is not a sign of flesh tone or variation in the coloring. How long, how much money, and how painful that darkening process was I simply cannot imagine.

He seems quite a nice fellow, welcoming me. I ask for a Maker's on the rocks and a water back. He complies with humor and aplomb. Smiles at me like I am an actual worthwhile inhabitant of the planet. I smile back, best I can. Clad as I am in a Hawaiian shirt, and too short, too clean khaki shorts. And Walgreen's flip-flops. He nods and turns to refill the pint of another guest.

I turn to my left. A very stark, but quite interesting youngish woman, brunette-banged and adorned with a bicep dragon, looks up from her cellphone. She lets her eyes stop on mine for the better part of a microsecond, pivots on her barstool, gets up, and moves to a table in the corner. Never breaking her telephonic conversational stream. It did not take her long to recognize, and dismiss, my sort.

Then that sort, me, leans forward on his stool, elbows on the bar, for what seems a long while, acting like he is watching the herd of mismatched dogs shuffling around sniffing ankles. Only occasionally glancing away from this diverting spectacle to watch the progress of an advancing women's soccer match on a large mural of an LED screen.

In the first scenario, a large black and white pit bull pairs with a brown Chihuahua the size of his head. Together they sniff a pair of sparkly-strapped five-inch heels containing an intriguingly turned ankle. In the other Norway is losing. Corner kick. Neither the owner of the ankles nor the Scandinavians recognize my interest.

There are no cats in attendance, I realize. This is Dog World, and no doubt about it.

I am amused, but somehow cannot seem to meld with this scene. Again totally my fault. I realize that I came here with a chip on my shoulder. I need to reset and try again. Reboot as a human being, get my passport validated as an ongoing

resident and part-owner of a portion of the Crescent City.

So, inevitably conceding my overly optimistic anticipation of immediate success, I decide to head back home.

As my hand goes up to open the exit door, I look at the clock on the wall alongside. Mistake. It turns out I was only happy for thirty-five minutes. What an effort for such a tiny portion of joy. Large sigh. I will do better, I promise myself. I must persevere.

I venture to cross the street. Where sits another, uh . . . less refined establishment.

The proprietors there seem to relish their own place in the unhip universe. For, beside the entrance, a sign is posted, plainly visible from the hipster bar:

"DRESS CODE IS STRICTLY ENFORCED:
FOUR TEETH MINIMUM."

There is a cat on the windowsill next to the door, mewing and lowering its head for a scratching. It seems at home. The almost-edible scent of burgers and bacon emanates from the interior.

It dawns on me once again: *"A-ha! None of this is actually important! I can be happy and have no rules. No penance. No categories.*

"Just like the cats.

"The *cats!"*

I feel reassured. I belong here, in New Orleans. With Ralph and Nigel. Who knew this all along, and are consummately happy all the time.

I must hurry home. It is almost suppertime, and I have some questions for those two.

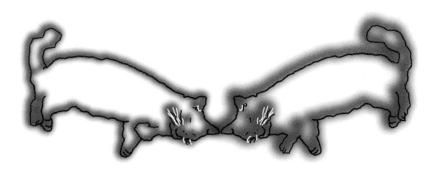

BAYOU ST JOHN

Le Punk aime voyager, il s'en fiche du comment

(The Punk Loves to Travel, He Doesn't Care How)

Punk'n listened happily as the transparent neon-blue waves splashed ashore one after another, the warm salt water creating a barely-audible happy-baby gurgle as it dissolved into the sugar white sand. Palm fronds rustled and glinted in the tropical sun, a breeze tilting the trees ever so slightly toward the *zocalo,* where a tiny carnival was setting up for the night hours' *paseo.*

There was the scent of lobsters being grilled with garlic, lime, sea salt, and chilies. It was the winter season, time for the *langosta* to march in the tens of thousands down the Yucatán Straits between Isla Mujeres and the Quintana Roo peninsula. Dozens of wooden boat bottoms and hundreds of plastic-draped restaurant tables were full of massive crustaceans. He did not actually know this, but he did.

Without interruption the shift occurred. His paws now walked the streets near *Abbesses,* the north-central Metro stop. Less than two blocks later, he was offered a version of feline heaven. On the north side of the street, spread out in display boxes embedded in ice and seaweed, were dozens upon dozens of the most enticing shellfish he had ever seen. Plus oysters. A dozen different types of oysters, and the same number of fresh fish, all calling out his name: *"Le Punk'n!"*

> *Brasserie La Mascotte* was the place, and they made prominent the sources of their name via a flyer attached to the menu, which translated as: *"Mascotte* (French noun) a late derivative of *'mascoto Provençal,'* indicating a bewitching or enchantment in game (1850), itself derived from *'masco,'* a sorceress, which originated from the ancient 'Provençal *masca'* (1396), mask."
> *"Vous devez visiter le quartier des Abbesses au printemps!"*

The cat had heard the human voice narration in both sequences. He even remembered that the musical human voice sounds in each were distinctly different. He had no idea what story they were telling, or how that story was logically relevant to him eating or being happy. Reasoning narratives did not matter in Pahoo travel. They were, however, couched in soothing and untroubled music, and voices undoubtedly describing sources of pleasure. That worked for him. He did not care to go deeper.

Punk'n enjoyed it all as he lounged on the back of his chair in New Orleans' *Faubourg Marigny.* He was in his element, a cat's world centered on warmth, comfort, and good food. Accompanied by a dearth of loud noises.

Le Punk, an orange tailless tabby, had acquired a sound and sight collection of comfortable images from the world that existed outside his house by osmosis, from a 55-inch LED screen left unattended at least eight hours a day, tuned to the Travel Channel. His humans left the sound on relatively high, and with the flickering images, maintained a fairly believable semblance of someone being home during the day. Punk'n didn't quite understand why they did this but, in his solution-wise feline instinct, suspected it was to keep Bad Cats out of the house while they were at work. Good Cats, like Punk'n, were welcome.

OK with him. He sat on the couch alone for many, many hours watching the screen, and he could call up and inhabit pawfuls of memories now, completely on his own. When not on the couch, he dozed in resonating quiet a few rooms away from the blaring TV, on his most comfy chair.

He had come to this home via an odd, life-threatening set of circumstances, and had now almost forgotten how bad things really were in his first seven weeks of life.

Out there.

He had little memory of his first humans, other than they were young creatures and moved about either very quickly and jerkily or very slowly and lethargically. They had paid five small pieces of paper for him, as the prime pick from a gutter punk's litter: "The one without a tail, maybe rare Manx blood there somewhere," they had said. "Three weeks old. Unweaned."

"Not our problem."

"Ten dollars."

"No."

"OK, five."

His young humans had stolen a metal spiked leather cat collar from a French Quarter corner store and fastened it securely around the young kitten's neck.

In the second week of his residence, just learning to eat solid food, he had found his humans laying out on the floor snoring, in an oddly scented room. The door was open. He walked out, fascinated by the sounds and smells of the street.

And was immediately lost. Which he did not realize until he got hungry and turned around to go back in for his bowl. He had no idea where he was.

He avoided screeching cars and human chasers for

almost two weeks, until one day he found himself hiding on a wide front porch near the Fair Grounds racetrack, cringing in a corner, cramping from lack of food, and wheezing because the ever-tightening collar had almost cut off his breathing. His rapid growth had also almost eliminated his ability to swallow.

A human came out the door onto the porch, and immediately began a soft, comforting kitten chant.

"It's OK, sweetie. Not going to hurt you. You look hungry. Would you like some food?" He slowly went back in the house, only to reemerge a minute or so later with something smelling exceedingly flavorsome in his fingers. The orange kitten could smell it. He approached the offering, sniffed it.

Licked it.

He was starving, but he started wheezing the moment he had a bite in his mouth. He could not get anything down his constricted throat.

The human saw this, went back inside, and returned with a pair of crisscrossed silvery implements. He gently reached down, rubbed the kitten's neck, inserted the tip of the scissors, and cut the collar through.

It fell off.

"*I can breathe!*" thought the baby orange tabby. "I can *eat!* And immediately consumed the entire portion the human had offered.

"Wait here just a second," said the man, leaving quietly, then returning with more food and a bowl of water.

The kitten decided right then that he was home. And the man decided the same thing.

"So, what shall we call you, Kitty? You looked rather like a punk rock cat with that spiked collar. Hmmmm. And you are as *orange* as a pumpkin! How about Punk'n?"

Punk'n. Born a second time into his very own life.

The Punk grew to love his home and the comforts that came with it and, for the first year of his habitation, seldom went outside even though there was both a protected front and backyard.

"I can see everything I need to see from my window," he thought.

Punk'n finally did calm down. His anxieties and nightmares faded, and he loosened up. More every day. He stopped being so nervous. The survival concerns of his feral days dwindled, and his worried mode of living dissipated.

He started spending time on the laps of his human couple as they sat in front of the TV eating their dinners each evening.

Thus he discovered TV.

And travel.

In a second Mexican episode, Punk'n drove with the TV through the pitch black of a dense rain forest. The Punk sensed the camera was once again seeking a meal. The quest was punctuated every few minutes by the swarming of lesser dog-like bats, *Peropteryx macrotis,* one of fifty-five species found on the Yucatan Peninsula, explains the narrator.

Punk'n did not understand these human sounds, of course, but found himself speculating that he would like to catch one of those flying rats. "Probably tasty," he thought.

There was no sign of humans or their electricity on either side of the road for what seemed like endless miles. The travelers babbled on in the car, as humans would, and another voice occasionally sounded from above to complement the auto conversation. Finally, there was a light. A beer sign, again went the narration, that lit up off and on, illuminating the edge of an ocean, pulsing ashore right behind.

As an avid viewer, Punk'n knew this was a turning point in the picture story.

The flickering light of beeswax candles was visible through the exterior walls of the structure. This was not a log cabin but a twig cabin, woven branches barely supported the palm frond roof.

"*A* scritchable sand floor!" For a cat of the Punk's sensibilities it was, in a word, "Perfect."

There were no other customers, and as the owner/chef/waiter emerged from the kitchen, he told the camera crew they were his first patrons in two days.

Punk'n could surmise this part from the scarcity of eateries in what looked to resemble his human's cooking and eating areas. The rest of the narrative he just watched and read in his own manner, reacting to movement and sound and the occasional cat-recognizable shape. It was part of the adventure for him, this human activity and communication.

"Maybe I will listen long enough and be able to understand human. I myself could never make such discordant noises, thinks the cat. Though it could be useful. Possibly."

He turned his head to be able to hear the sounds better as the narrative continued.

The man explained unapologetically that he never felt any pressure to bring in lots of people, and thereby lost his restorative siesta time. It was too bad that Punk'n couldn't understand this part of the discussion, as his empathy for both the chef and the place would have tripled immediately.

"There is something gentle, deeply understanding and catlike about the energetic little cook," thought the Punk, even without absorbing the meaning of the notions he was entertaining.

"We'd probably get along just fine, especially with all those fish right outside his back door."

The owner was happy to see the TV show crew, nonetheless. And to make his happiness evident, he brought out a bottle of clear liquid and four glasses — one for him, of course — to celebrate the joy of the visit.

Then he announced that he had the makings of two dishes in the kitchen that would match the happiness of the event.

He had started a Yucatecan-style *pollo pibil* earlier in the day, which should now be ready. The sounds *PO-YO PEE-BEEL*, register with the Punk. "Poyo peebeel, hm. Sounds good. I wonder what it will mean? And what will it taste like?"

These were chickens from the owner's yard next door, which he had killed and dressed at daybreak, coated with Mayan honey from his own hives and orange juice from his citrus trees. They were wrapped in banana leaves cut from the plants bordering the road in front of the restaurant. He demonstrated his actions and gestured to explain.

Punk'n began to understand that food was indeed involved. He had been right all along. This was one of the reasons he loved these programs so much. The solving of the puzzle.

These *pollos* he had buried in coconut shell coals that morning and left cooking for the day, and should now have roasted and melded with all the flavors. He said they were large birds, each enough for two hungry people.

The owner's brother, who he pointed out was at this very moment sitting on a bench in the kitchen and waving to the camera, also with a glass of liquid in his other hand, had that afternoon caught a two-pound *huachinango*, a red snapper, and he would fry it whole in coconut oil, along with some *papas fritas,* French fries. And he will accompany that dish with a salad of cabbage and home-grown tomatoes dressed with mild chilies, lime juice, and sea salt. And, of course, the customary half-kilo of yellow corn tortillas.

The camera crew and host finished the bottle — and the chicken and the fish and tortillas — and ended up shaking hands, laughing loudly, and slapping backs in the kitchen some three hours later, still the only guests of the evening.

The video became more erratic and bumpy as the evening progressed, and though Punk'n could not tell, the host was slurring his words.

Later the visitors drove off slowly, camera still rolling to capture the chef's repeated calls of *"Vaya con Dios,"* and headed out into the bat-filled night.

The complete story had eluded him. Nonetheless, the Punk was gratified. He was intrigued again by the flavors and smells that might come with *Poyo peebeel.* He hoped that the can of choice for his dinner that eve would be fish or chicken, to complement the food he had just seen eaten in a comforting foreign clime.

Meanwhile this new bit of travel needed to be digested in a deep long nap. He decided to get on the human bed and snuggle in amidst the half dozen pillows that occupied the top of that structure.

Among all the things he had come to enjoy about his adopted home, he most loved travel, human laps, and the human-manufactured lap substitutes: pillows.

Punk'n loved diving in amidst pillows.

He imagined a world filled with them.

And maybe a *poyo peebeel* or two.

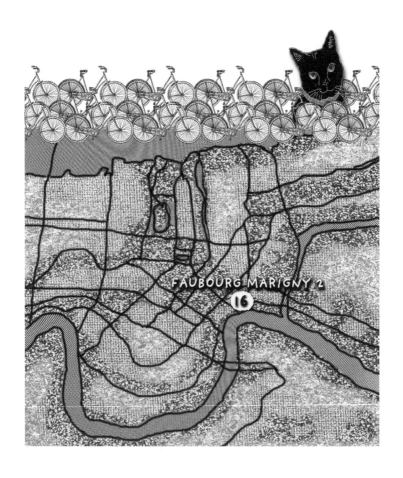

FAUBOURG MARIGNY 2

16

Buddhi devient une attraction touristique
(Buddhi Becomes a Tourist Attraction)

"Skrreeeeeee-kawk!"

"Skreeeee, POP! . . . -dies and gentlemen . . . just to get you oriented before we take off . . . kawk kawk kawk . . . would like to give you an idea of the nature of the area through which we will be . . . SKREEEE! . . ."

". . . kawk!! . . . as the houses on many of these streets are indicative of the Caribbean influences rampant in the *Faubourg Marigny*," assertively spouts the dull-blonde, white-visored Guide. The volume of his battery-powered pocket amplifier finally adjusted, he now moves into the mental mode necessary for an evocative full-bore script regurgitation.

He pulls his eye-shade down over his brow so he won't have to visually interact with his fellow cyclists. He has

119

been brought on board as an unpaid intern by the tour company partly based on his perceived skills in non-confrontation. No one in this mobile street theatre will ever feel threatened, at least not by its principal Actor/Guide. No refunds after the tour begins is the rule, in any case.

Having begun, the Guide confidently leans his bicycle to the side and braces his left foot on the curb, this to allow for broad gestures in the time-tested physical *méthode* of a classically-trained thespian.

And now properly situated, he continues his memorized monologue.

"Bold colors juxtaposed on lacy architectural filigrees are a recurring motif in single, double, camelback, and full two-story shotgun houses of the mid-nineteenth century. You will notice a mix of Greek and Roman Revival houses, and the rare Moorish influence, all interspersed among French, Spanish, and turn of the twentieth century American Arts & Crafts styles . . ."

Frank hears this narration from behind the drawn lace curtains, which mask the house interior, and himself, from view. He can see that the Guide is wearing a small headset, secured behind his right ear. Two efficient and quite loud speakers are attached, one to each of the front panels of his equally loud fluorescent green vest. On the back of which is redundantly affixed "GUIDE" in large plastic orange letters.

The city's commercial tourism industry asserts that the French Quarter is romantically called the *Vieux Carré,* but doesn't mention that Vieux Carré doesn't mean "French Quarter." It translates as "Old Square." And looking at the two-wheeled crowd assembled outside his window, Frank can see nothing but a gaggle of bicycles without the horizontal bar, equipped with very wide seats and fat white-walled tires.

"Merriam, come over here and look at this!" yells a cycle-mounted Husband to a similarly-situated Wife. It is their first-ever bicycle tour: their individual safety helmets are somehow on backwards. It must also be their first-ever visit to New Orleans: they seem to hope that Frank's Craftsman house may indeed qualify as Moorish. The couple is obviously on a quest for the exotic, wearing beach-style apparel on what locals would consider a freakishly cold late spring morning — 53 degrees Fahrenheit. Snow boot weather down south. Much of their accompanying wheeled tribe is similarly clad, accentuated by a preference among the males for hard shoes and black polyester socks as an accompaniment for thick leg hair emerging from under garishly patterned shorts. Massive elastically-supported shelves of pale cleavage seeking the sun is *de rigueur* for the females. Tan lines being much cheaper and more effective than lingerie for arousing a chilled Midwestern male back home.

". . . however," continues the Guide, while looking at the house in front of the group, Frank and Buddhi's home, "much of this neighborhood has declined in recent years, and there are a few slightly scruffy 'modern' properties intruding amidst the treasures."

"Scruffy," he had said, setting Frank smoldering once again. Unknown to him when he bought it twenty years prior, his house was indeed aluminum-sheathed.

And "modern." "Does 1890 qualify as modern?"

"Yes, I know, I know," he tells Buddhi. "Anyone who

has lived here more than a day can testify to the fact that yesterday was better. The Marigny has not maintained itself well physically in these rough times.

"But we still qualify as scenic enough to warrant hourly out-of-town visitor impositions, walking, bicycling, on Segways, in carriages. Pausing at our homes to discuss them. And every guide who transits the streets can be heard announcing loudly to his or her paid listeners of the neighborhood's 'majestic past.' Unfortunately, such compliments are inevitably followed with a qualifying phrase: '. . . though it is obviously not now as it once was.'

"Or: 'Scruffy.'" This just said while standing directly in front Frank and Buddhi's place of residence.

Frank had heard.

"It's like having an internet comment section tagged onto your actual real-world life.

"Scruffy, my mule-drawn ass," he finds himself muttering downward. "I have put up with this as long as possible. It is time for action.

"Buddy, come here, please," Frank again says toward the floor, from which emerges the sleek black feline, who raises his chin.

"Mowt," Buddhi says with some vigor, knowing that he may get picked up and administered abdominal rubs as a consequence of answering Frank's call. The human does this, and also massages Buddhi's ears as a reward for his attention.

"Mowt, mowt," the cat says in acknowledgment of his favorite reinforcement.

Frank is now ready.

He takes a deep breath, grabs his pre-printed visual aid, opens the front door and, still carrying the cat, emerges onto the front porch. The Guide immediately winces and stops speaking, his verbal locomotive now derailed.

This is not the first time Frank has intruded on the Guide's lecture. Frank tries to do this as often as possible, responding forcefully when these people sully his ordinary though comforting existence.

Buddy remains calm and purring, even as Frank suddenly yells, *"Ola, turistas!"* ("Forgive me, please," Frank thinks, "but in these divisive and paranoid days, I divide my admittedly microcosmic world into two divisions — neighbors and tourists. I recognize this as an indefensible prejudice on my part, but that does not deter me.")

In the hand not surrounding Buddy, Frank's left, he now holds forward a large printed sign. "PICTURESQUE LOCAL & COLORFUL PET," it reads, with an arrow currently pointing up at the cat and Frank's face.

"DONATION SUGGESTED," it says below the first lines. Then, in smaller letters: "PET REQUIRES REGULAR SUSTENANCE."

"Aw, a kitty," says the Wife, undoubtedly a viewer of the most heinous "cute cat" YouTube obscenities.

Frank props his signage upright on the outlying bottom ledge of the porch column.

He now take his own turn at public speaking, raising his voice in a much-contemplated though completely extemporized bit of verbal mayhem: "Two-wheeled wanderers of America. You've heard about *Jericho* and *Jackass 2,*" he begins. "You have heard about the Great Wall of China and the fully-loaded flame-grilled Whopper! You have heard about the 'Midnight Rambler'!"

"Uhhhh . . ." articulates the Wife.

"What the . . . ?" questions the Husband.

But the homeowner is quickly finding his oratorical groove: "I come to you today in awe of those benchmarks of human intellectual achievement, and in simultaneous reverence to the beating heart of our beloved but occasionally . . . *scruffy* . . . neighborhood."

Frank is channeling his inner preacher: "For it is written," he exclaims, raising the stakes, moving into the vocal tone of a major pulpit sermon. "In the scruffy shall ye find the rewards of eternal bliss! And don't you want bliss? Isn't that what we all want, even while vacationing in an overpriced time-share?"

"Damn right!" yells a portly and particularly hirsute gentleman in the rear ranks of cyclists. He is the width of Texas and the height of Rhode Island.

"Thank you, sir. I feel justified," Frank tells him, righteously.

"Three hunnerd-fitty bucks a goddamn night and the bathroom light don' work! They's chewin' gum under the dinin' room tabletop. An' the fridge smells like some homeless Ay-rab sheep been doin' his business in there. An' I don' mean no oil futures. Nope, ain't none a that bliss shit goin' on in this burg, for damn sure."

"Now, Bert," says the woman next to him, who then turns to address me, "that's his thyroid meds talkin', mister. He likes this place."

"The hell I do! Casino is rigged and the nekkid bars got a passel a' retired grammaws takin' off they clothes. Cain't git yer money's worth nowhere."

Frank replies, quietly but fervently: "You can from me, kind sir. *Lordhavemercy,* yes!" He is feeling it, really feeling the latent pulpit-juicer in himself this time. He extends his hand, reverentially.

In response, the Husband awkwardly penguin-walks his bicycle across the sidewalk, reaches for his wallet, extracts and extends a rumpled dollar bill across the fence toward Frank, cringing back and releasing his hold as Frank walks forward and touches the bill with the already-full cat hand, his right.

Merriam takes a picture of her husband's charitable action with her phone.

"Mowt," repeats Buddhi once he sees the currency has been

passed. He has once again intelligently connected the sight of these small greenish pieces of paper with the subsequent appearance of Kitty Deluxe Mediterranean Seafood Dinner.

Such an intelligent creature, this.

The couple seems to have been unoffended by either the earlier "turista" label or Frank's spiel, and genuinely happy to have paid the price of admission to a drama featuring the inner workings of a complex Southern micro-society. That being Buddhi and the homeowner.

The Husband continues to stare at the two New Orleans residents with his mouth, in mid-seventeenth century literary terminology, agape.

Once again Frank does look somewhat like an unmade bed this morning, even he must admit. He is wearing yesterday's rather wrinkled jeans and a "Defend New Orleans" t-shirt in anticipation of quiet computer work, but he resolutely believes that he deserves to be regarded as "picturesque" nonetheless.

However, Buddhi may not scientifically qualify as "colorful," as the resident cat is in reality a completely colorless pallet of velvety midnight black.

Frank discovers that the Wife, undismayed, is admiring the digital photograph she has taken of the aforementioned two locals receiving economic support from her brave and daring spouse. He is sure that she is thinking that this moment frozen in time will be a definite keeper in the computer slideshow back home this coming month, displayed on the wall of a knickknack-filled living room in a house surrounded by also frozen snow drifts.

Frank usually demands further remuneration when an image is captured of his roommate and his own visage, but the moment has passed for additional solicitation.

The Guide frowns, recovers his composure, shakes his head and says, "Moving on . . ."

"I have now done my part. Maybe next time he won't stop here again," Frank tells Buddhi.

"Mowt!"

And, on that prompting, Frank returns to his kitchen to provide sustenance to his "colorful" accomplice.

Another, even happier "Mowt!" resounds.

ST CHARLES AVENUE
UPTOWN
17

Rentrer à la Maison
(To Go Home)

Dale enjoyed the walk to his car after teaching his classes at the university, but on this lovely, simple Friday afternoon he was not expecting an encounter with longing and fulfillment. And, of course, he was not expecting a personal dialogue with a cat.

The untenured professor could not afford parking on campus, so he opted for a daily search for a spot on the avenue, a grand colonnade of mansions and massive live oak trees. The beauty of the setting made up for the discomforts of a six- to seven-block walk after a day filled with the demands of unruly, self-inflated, rich kids reeking of pheromones.

Today he was shedding the stress of academia once again, listening to the birds chirp and the automatic lawn sprinklers distributing a sparkling cloud of undrinkable New Orleans water across manicured yards.

So he was surprised when there appeared, sitting upright on the sidewalk opposite where he was parked in the middle of the block, a large, though quite skinny, feline. Irregularly black-spotted but mostly white, with a large head and an expressive face. He was staring straight at Dale as he approached, walking eastward on St. Charles Avenue from the end of the block, nearest school.

When Dale spotted him, he clicked his tongue as he so often did when requesting the attention of his own cats, Persephone and Paulinho.

This stranger kitty responded immediately, first standing still, and then walking slowly toward the human. Actively speaking with every step. "Mrahht, mraahhht, *OW,*" he said loudly.

He stopped at Dale's feet and sat again, at ease, still looking directly into his face.

"Mroooo*owwwt,*" he said with conviction.

Dale bent over, trying all the while not to drop his bag, and scratched his head.

"Mrowt."

Dale understood him completely, and nodded his own head.

Then he paused, realizing how crazy that seemed. "He is waiting for something," he thought.

"He is waiting for me to ask him into the car.

"He wants to Go Home."

Thinking this, Dale looked again at the newly-introduced cat, and said out loud, this time more personally, "Nice to meet you, my boy." For it was most certainly a him. "He is not just another stray," thought Dale. "Though he is indeed skinny, his coat is clean and shiny. He has no collar, but he is most assured around people and knows how to communicate what he wants.

"I can feel this cat. I know we are comrades, have the same struggles. I know him.

"He must be someone's kitty. Must be. Even if he is lost,

what can I do to help him to his own home? Put him in my car and post notices in this neighborhood?

"And what will I do in the meantime? Surprise Alice and take him to my place, a house already occupied by two very territorial cats, and tell them both that this new guy is just there temporarily, and they should remain calm and not start pissing on everything to mark their reserved spots?

"Could I try to sequester him in my backyard office while I try to find him a different home?

"But I am just standing here, still, looking at this cat. I have no food to offer as compensation for my inability to do as he asks, and if I leave, he will probably just disappear."

He walked to the side of the car, opened the door, and threw his bag in. The cat had turned to face the car and the street, and watched intently.

Dale decided he must speak: "Just go home, kit. You will be fine. I can't take you with me." He realized again that he was talking to a cat. Again. Trying to reason with this particular one.

"Mroo*owwwt.*"

He got in the door, closed it, started the engine, and began to do the necessary U-turn to head home. The cat did not move, stayed in place, and continued to watch intently.

As Dale got into the opposite lane and started to accelerate away, he looked back again. The cat was still there watching.

He wanted to Go Home.

Dale drove there, home, alone and tried not to look back, tried not to think.

Weeks later he did, and explained it to his wife Alice, who had been wondering why he had dropped so suddenly into a long sky of sadness-filled clouds. Stratocumulus. She had not wanted to bother him, or make it worse, so she waited patiently until he felt ready to speak.

He sat now on the couch, with a cat on either side of him, rubbing ears while he settled himself. Persephone and Paulinho purred, reassuring him. It was time to get what he had been thinking out into the open.

Dale wanted to detail what he had been feeling during those weeks to his family, but found it hard finding a starting place.

Then he realized what it was. The street kit.

"I never saw him again, but to this day, he has haunted me.

"He is probably fine. My loss, any way you look at it. And for some reason I hurt for him.

"I wish I had done something more to help. Not a very good or strong adult, me.

"But there is a larger issue than this one kit. I do not know why I have become so affected by encounters with other creatures. Why I am at times so reluctant to invest in yet another emotional attachment of any sort.

"You would think that all these cats, and humans, I have encountered over the years would have taught me — what with all their many comings and goings — that the arrival and departure mechanism is just the way of things.

"There is a brief window of cognizant life. You enter, enjoy it, eat the kibbles and the bits, and then you are gone. It should be so simple to allow, and then let go of, attachments.

"It is not.

"As a concrete result of this ongoing life punctuated by feline encounters, I still refuse to confess to becoming another crazy bag man, some smelly derelict lost to society, surrounded in later life only by uncontrolled dozens of mewling and pissing creatures. The stereotype is not always the case.

"I am not so smelly. Not yet.

"Sometimes you just have to project the good and the positive, however nebulous, and let life gather.

"Life is, drawn to it.

"It comes to the doorstep, willing to exchange love for love. Or maybe tuna bits.

"And that is a damn good thing."

"Yes it is," said Alice.

Persephone and Paulinho continued to purr, but even louder. They had recognized the word "tuna."

Citrine fait face à l'univers
(Citrine Deals with the Universe)

"Aloof" was a grudgingly accurate emotional and physical adjective for describing Citrine. She has been with her humans for seven years, and seldom in all that time has she come to ground. In any sense.

As the last arrival in a multi-feline Napoleon Avenue household, she immediately felt threatened by all the other cats, so she spent her initial days and nights on fence tops, rooftops, and atop branches in the avocado tree out back.

The habit stuck.

But getting her food and water, and affection, was quite difficult, as she refused to budge from her perches. It was actually a wise decision. The other two females in the household did *not* want her indoors, or even on the ground *outside* their house. It was theirs. First Cats had rights of priority, after all.

So the two softhearted and inventive Johnsons, homeowners Rhonda and Ted, connived and collaborated to get meals safely to Citrine. They stapled strips of velcro on many of her nesting spots, so that the oppositely-textured velcro on her food dishes might be placed up above, and remain unmoving, on branches and fence posts.

It worked. There, with bowl attached to branch, she ate in peace. Citrine appreciated that effort on her behalf, and consumed her food often and heartily. Maybe too heartily, remarked Ted, as the dainty tree-climber had expanded substantially waist-wise over the last few years. Her agility was nearly compromised on the leafy tightropes she walked, he thought.

And so Ted had been paying attention to ingredients listed on packaging, and tracked fat content in the food he presented to her. So far she had not noticed any lack of flavor in her meals. And the quantity she consumed has remained constant.

Citrine also adored being petted, but not in the presence of the other cats, as she feared, rightly, that it would escalate their enmity toward her. In any case, administering kitty-love when perched precariously amidst a sprawling tree on a short metal ladder could be difficult, but was always rewarding, as the Johnsons told visitors from their own experience.

Observing the feeding of Citrine had become something of a required pre-meal show for the couple's Uptown human dinner guests, with attendant oohs and ahhhs and occasional hand-clapping for the procedure. This did not diminish the feline's appetite. If anything, she cleaned her bowl more completely in front of an audience.

Citrine had thus become something of a celebrity in the surrounding neighborhood, and the Johnsons were often approached amidst the pet-care aisles of the Napoleon Avenue supermarket by neighbors inquiring as to the health of the "tree kitty."

Citrine. A star. In many ways.

After all, the Johnsons had named her after a semiprecious stone known as "the light maker." It was not an easy path when they first began looking for a moniker for the free-spirited bundle of fur. When Rhonda, a deep-diver in numerous "alt" philosophies and possibilities, was first searching for a name, she began opening arcane texts, thinking there might be some intuitive clue to be found there.

During one particular morning of dusty page-turning, she stumbled into *An Enlightened Approach to Astro-Gemological Brainwave Behavior,* which included a list of precious stones and their attributes, in terms of psychological interaction, to living beings.

At this point, Citrine came *ohsoclose* to being named "Lapis." Surname: Lazuli.

Oooo, no, please.

But at that very intuitive and decisive moment, Rhonda chanced to look up into the yard, and instantly was smiling and laughing with the young kitten's continued tree-climbing escapades. Returning her gaze to the reference book's open pages, her eye caught the phrase *"Citrine, the bringer of light, positivity and joy,"* describing the bright yellow stone.

And that was that.

The golden-eyed, dark black cat with the faint orange-yellow star on her forehead was named for light and happiness.

Citrine, most certainly.

And, so named, she slept happily under the stars each night, considering the shining universe above as her personal expansive ceiling. She thought that since all the other cats stayed inside from dinner until breakfast, the night sky was solely her possession.

But her humans began having a few misgivings. After a few years of operating in this fashion, climbing each morning and night to serve cat meals, drawbacks became apparent to the humans enmeshed in the system. One major fly in the ointment was that Citrine, and the Johnsons, had to deal with her rainy day mealtimes.

On more than one occasion Ted was enlisted to convey breakfast to the damp but still insistent tree-sitting cat in the driving rain.

This also required that he stand there on the metal ladder amidst cracks of thunder and flashes of lightning, holding an umbrella over Citrine and her dish for the ten minutes or so it took her to finish her slightly moistened food.

Ted did not come in from such meteorological experiences in a pleasant mood.

"We've got to get Citrine down to earth," he vowed one particularly stormy night. "I'm a lightning rod out there. A lightning rod with pending pneumonia."

"But dear," Rhonda reminded him, "she has no territory of her own. And if she leaves the tree or the fence top, the other cats attack her. She goes next door under the neighbor's house when the rain and cold come, but she can't get her food under there."

"Then we will get Citrine her own house."

It was not an easy process. True, they owned the house and the lot on which it stood already. There was a space

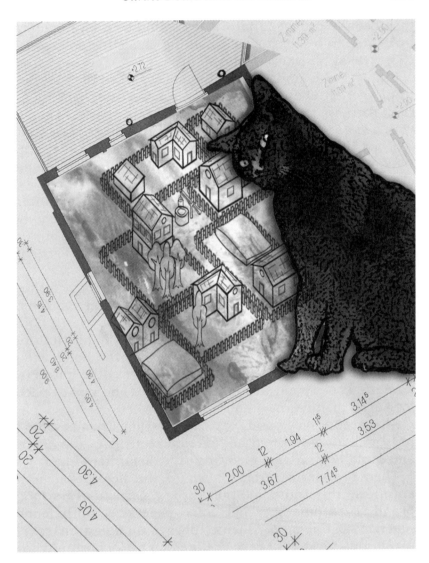

on top of a tallish planter, well out of sight of the sidewalk, that would allow for the a small cat-sized structure, and still be slightly out of the established domains of the other four-legged residents.

But finding a suitable cat-house, and going through the trouble of construction and placement, all without the absolute promise that Citrine would be even remotely interested in being "inside" anything, made the Johnsons' effort feel at times, well, almost futile.

Still, Ted was undaunted. Rhonda searched the internet until she felt she could search no more, and right then, right then, there it was. The perfect size, the perfect shape, with a viewing deck for a roof, front and side windows that relieved the sense of confinement, and a small plate atop the door with a crescent moon. Which reflected the shape of Citrine's own eyes.

The house arrived in a flat cardboard carton after only three days. In the company of a ten-page assembly manual. "Is this in English? Is it?" Ted inquired to no one in particular. It was not. It was in Chinese-inflected French, with diagrams that may have well been in Sanskrit.

He started the assembly. In English, with some rather crude Anglo-Saxonisms thrown in, as time and again his hammer found knuckle rather than nailhead.

After three smashed fingernails, a splinter in his thumb, and a rather painful Chinese paper cut, the house was complete. The couple worked together to put the house in a secure spot, line it with a cozy blanket, and make space for a food dish on the stoop.

All it needed now was a kitty. That evening Rhonda waited until well after all the other cats had finished eating, and she could hear Citrine meowing outside for her dinner.

Then the clever human went to the new house and sprinkled the entire interior with a particularly strong brand of catnip. She had some experience with feline reaction to the herb. Citrine, always standing on some precarious roost, had never before had the opportunity for exposure to the happy effects of the shredded green leaves.

Rhonda carried Citrine and her dinner to the secure site. She carefully placed the cat inside and let her get a nose full. Citrine sniffed, then sniffed harder, and finally licked up a mouthful. Her eyes began to dilate, she *meowed* as if in heat, and proceeded to roll around in a most undignified manner. She exhaled and just lay there for a moment, looking about.

Inside her own safe space.

Rhonda watched for a few moments longer, not wishing to embarrass her beloved cat by witnessing such lascivious mannerisms.

She put the food dish down, just outside the door.

She knew that the stimulated/sedated Citrine would all-too-soon regain her appetite.

She did. With a post-stimulant vengeance.

Later that evening, with the stars once again out and shining, Citrine peeked out her front window and realized that her private universe was all around, not just at the treetops.

All she had to do was look.

Citrine finally had come to earth.

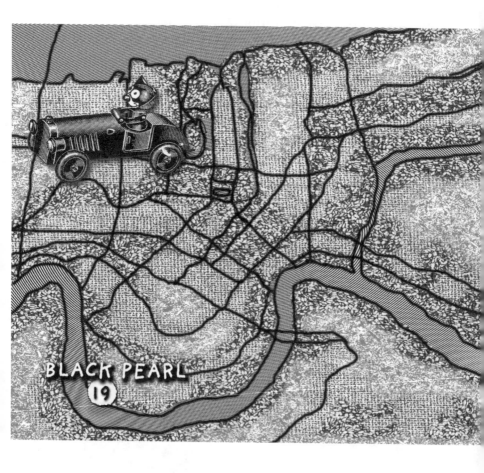

BLACK PEARL
19

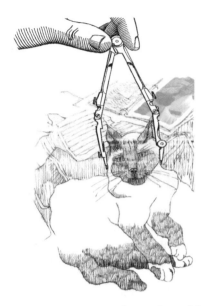

Norman, en traduction
(Norman, in Translation)

Violette Fontaine studied law at the university law school near Audubon Park *aux Etats-Unis,* so that she could also have the opportunity to practice the profession in France. It seemed that contemporary French and Louisiana legalese were still based on the same Napoleonic Code.

So, as they said on the banks of both the Seine and lower Mississippi, *"Tout ce qui fonctionne."* "Whatever works" had indeed been Violette's approach to living, all along.

She had pursued her bachelor's degree in French since, as a child living a mere single swamp west of the city, her Cajun and Creole neighbors all spoke variations of the language. Plus the idea of specializing in "Romance" languages appealed to the young high school grad. And then there was the fact that the lines at the university on the first day of freshmen registration were shortest for that particular romantic field of study.

Her mindset was different three and a half years later — she graduated early — so different that she took that final spring and summer off to "get serious" about law school. That decided, she found a semi-livable flat in the Black Pearl neighborhood, to be close to the university for study, and to be surrounded by a profusion of restaurants for work.

From that moment on, she planned her every move.

Mlle Fontaine often spoke out loud when juggling thoughts about her future, as in: *"Je peux travailler comme avocat."* I can work as a lawyer, utilizing a university degree, which I paid for by slaving as a very common waitress in tourist haunts. Or, I can make an uncommon living by taking my clothes off and dancing at a place like the Moulin Rouge, again for tourists, but with a body I got for free.

"Ça ñ'a pas d'importance pour moi."

And it truly did not matter to her. The choice of occupation was unimportant.

She was, in this case, speaking directly to her cat, Norman, as she also often did when seeking advice from a higher authority. "Or . . . maybe I should go to The Crazy Horse. The girls there don't have to wear stiff suits and ties, or much at all, and they get body-painted. That's being artfully naked, you know, Norm. *Comprends-tu, ma bien-aimée?"*

"Meh," he replied. In his own way, of course, understanding completely. Though he never quite knew how to respond when Violette got so intense.

She was indeed highly intelligent, and truly comfortable with a most lithe and compelling figure, a form that flowed uniformly over six feet of height. Violette Fontaine was gifted with a singularly attractive countenance, green eyes embellished with gold radial flashes, and a shock of red hair that swished about when she danced.

Dancing, which she also did quite provocatively, was one of her major pleasures. And a pleasure to others in her proximity, when she did dance.

But besides these physical attributes, Violette had

throughout her life managed to maintain a very strong and active sense of self, rooted in her logically-defined goals and the will and ability to find her own way to them.

She rightly surmised that either of her proposed Gallic occupations would work quite well for her purposes. She believed most strongly in the feasibility of her chosen options.

But there was another factor involved: Violette also lived with this cat.

Norman had been her sole companion and confidante throughout the rigors of law school. And in return for his constancy, she had promised that most unique and furry Siamese that he could travel along and reside with her in Europe, whichever way she ended up making a living. She would not leave him behind.

Norman had, after all, stayed with her and supported all her moods, through the academic tedium and the even more intense stress of bar exams.

This mutual residence took place in a very tiny apartment, in a very, very old building. It was stuccoed and balconied, a Franco-Hispanic anomaly covered in bright orange historically-inappropriate paint, crumbling into chalky white at the edges. All the while loudly advertising the fact that it was completely out of place in a neighborhood full of high-peaked Anglo rooflines and white porch columns.

Violette had speculated that, sometime in the nineteenth century, an expatriate Downtown French Catholic New Orleanian had bought the small lot and simply refused to conform with the housing modes of his Uptown American Protestant neighbors. If he was French, his home would reflect that fact.

"This is New Orleans, after all," she reasoned. *"C'est vrai."* Truly.

But over the last century or so, the streets just off South Carrollton Avenue that bounded Violette and Norman's Uptown home also evolved into a quick detour to avoid the larger avenue's slow stoplights. In recent years, the corner had become overwhelmed by automobile traffic, especially at morning and afternoon drive times.

Consequently, since he was a kitten, Norman had been raised entirely indoors. Which meant that he was, also consequently, paranoid of all the various and sundry noisy and bright and smelly and hot and cold elements of the outside world.

He reassured himself that he was, under all his nonchalance, most curious about the noisy and bright everything out there in moderation. And he pledged that at some point he would have the opportunity to see everything that was not included in his minuscule three rooms.

"There couldn't be that much else of value out there," he mused. "I just have to sit tight and it will be fine. Me and the girl. *C'est juste!*" Norman only took the trouble to reason his way out of his most immediate feline concerns.

Violette on the other paw had given a great deal of thought to their future, and had taken the time to school Norman extensively for this proposed life abroad. She spoke to him frequently, throughout the hours when she could spend her downtime thinking without guilt of something other than law. In French.

She remembered once again that he had been her sole companion as she studied and memorized the vagaries of the two highly suspect Napoleonic legal systems, each seemingly based on density of spices and the aromatic nature of required comestibles. Not human reason, *"pas la logique humaine,"* she emphasized to him, as she always did when she meant a phrase to be important.

"Meh," said the cat.

Norman had over the years grown to respond most easily to the human voice solely when he was addressed in French. He even spoke a word or two of the language himself.

"Miaou," he would say, *en française,* when the mood struck him as proper.

To which Violette would always respond: *"Je comprends totalement."* And she did. Understand completely, usually, the musings of her feline companion.

That is, when he spoke them aloud. Otherwise he was something of a mystery. As cats are wont to be, of course, but Norman, oh Norman, he could be one really big question mark.

She was pretty sure he cared for her. Or at least her can-opening abilities. Beyond that, she was a tad baffled. But remained resolute that she would repay his devotion to her by taking him to France.

So she did.

Though there were last minute obstacles. When US Customs asked about her *méthode de transport du chat,* she was forced to take some of her very hard-earned cash the morning of the flight and buy him an airline-legal cat carrier.

Before this, on less epic crosstown journeys, she had always carried him to the vet wrapped around her shoulders, with his head buried in her hair behind her left ear. All the while erratically driving her ancient Fiat Spider 124 convertible with the top down. She did this on purpose, the top down, not the erratic driving, because

Norman especially did not like the wind on his face. This meant a much easier transport, as he would not protest when she was close. He hid his head in V's flowing mane on these trips, only occasionally *miaou*-ing in her ear while being moved place to place.

Violette knew that he would remain firmly ensconced on her shoulders, steadfastly refusing to look out, until he felt himself safely inside a quiet space. Norman would then allow himself to be lulled by the calming muzak and the muted light of the veterinarian's enclosed office.

Thus was the vet allowed to proceed without the infliction of claw or tooth wounds. Violette had taught the doctor to use a few rudimentary French phrases in his examinations, to make these medical visits safer and less stressful, for all concerned.

For years Norman had not been ready for much more of the Outside World than that.

And now suddenly he was enclosed in a plastic box with a barred door. He had been purposely sedated, and was staring through that metal grill at as much sight and sound and smell as he had ever imagined. As if in a dream.

A dream that held Violette's voice pleading and wheedling a costumed stranger standing behind a tall desk to arrange his suitability as "carry-on," whatever that meant. He heard the sounds, but had no idea how they could, or would, affect him. He could hear only the harsh grind of English at this point, and the only thing getting through his befogged kitty perception was that he was sleepy.

Good thing, that.

He drank some water when Violette opened his door at an intermediate stop, in the process giving him another pill to calm his anxieties, and when next he woke completely he was being carried through an experience that was unimaginable to him just a few hours earlier. Norman was in Paris. Fully.

He did have the buffer of a few days bumping about, watched over by *sa copine,* his girl, while overcoming the lingering effects of the sedatives, in a very cheap single room of *une auberge.* But shortly thereafter Norman found himself being carried from the hostel, wrapped by Violette in a colorful harness and leash, and again placed around her shoulders for safe travel. He perched there willingly, his cold nose touching her cheek, rendered into a decorative feline boa.

Thus situated, they roamed the byways of the City of Light.

In some ways it was nowhere near as frightening an experience as he might have imagined. Here, for instance, everyone spoke his home language.

So he interacted, and spoke back, frequently, as they walked along. *"Que se passe-t-il?!?"* someone would

exclaim, seeing the cat. *"Rronronner,"* Norman would reply, as he knew quite well how to purr in French. *"Rronronner!"*

The Siamese turned quite a few heads as he cruised the streets on the shoulder of his companion, a stunningly beautiful redhead wearing an even redder béret. Who herself turned quite a few on her own merits. Norman was cued by the familiar language sounds to react, and he happily responded by lecturing passersby on the state of his feline world. He had never spoken this much at home, Violette realized, and she felt much empowered about her own residency by her cat's seeming ease of adaptation.

For Norman had quickly forgotten how scared he had been, as he now concentrated on transmitting his feline commentary to events that he perceived as worthwhile in this new place.

"Mi-euuuux," he would say, quite loudly, over the noises being transmitted by trains passing under the sidewalk métro grates.

Everyone hearing his ongoing vocalizations stopped, stared, and smiled when he spoke.

"*Ce chat est tellement mystérieux!*" he frequently heard in return, different words every time, of course, but the same transmission of human feeling. Indeed, he was. Very mysterious, especially to the unusually nonplussed Parisians he passed on the *Rue du Faubourg Saint-Honoré.*

He could sense their rather crude fascination, a genuine human generation of cat empathy, even if the actual meanings of the words they spoke went right by him.

He understood these French people.

"*Miaou!*" he exclaimed, feeling quite at home on the sidewalks of Paris. "*Woo-oo-ow!*"

Norman spoke the language.

He was going to like it here.

Monsieur B et son nom de neuvième quartier

(Mr. B & His Ninth Ward Name)

The malevolent water was alive and chasing him, it seemed. Time and time again he scampered away from the wind-driven, ever-blackening line of waves, only to find himself still standing belly-deep and being pushed off his feet by the current.

He was tiring, and didn't know how much longer he could fight these surprisingly aggressive elements and stay alive. He hadn't eaten, or swallowed any potable water, in two days. And now in the hours since the sun had come up, he had found himself in a constant struggle to keep his head above the oily, stinking fluid, which was rapidly filling every spot of high ground.

Then he saw it. A massive oak on the grounds of Holy Cross college, with its lower branches actually touching and rooting in the ground. He used his claws to climb up quickly, and within just a few minutes had found a high perch on the leeward side of the tree encircled by branches. The wind was less here, too, as this New Orleans neighborhood's levees arched northward to accommodate the Industrial Canal, deflecting the full force of the hurricane.

It was there that the boat full of volunteer veterinarians found him, two days later, shivering and weak. They fed him and hydrated him, checked him for disease or injury, then after twelve hours' rest in a carrier, when he had gained some strength back, they gave him protective inoculations, gradually put him into a quiet sleep, "fixed" him and clipped off the top of his right ear.

Their actions were not as callous as they sound. The National Guard, State Police, and NOPD had been instructed to euthanize — kill — all feral animals in the city on sight. Many had been poisoned by the water, were sickened by the waste in which they were living, or just made insane by the lack of food. The reasoning was that removing one more threat could only help the humans returning to their homes.

The volunteers had let the authorities know what they would be doing, and that if they spotted an animal with a clipped right ear they could be assure that that particular animal, though homeless, at least was healthy and uninfected. And therefore should not be killed.

The only problem was that after stabilizing the rescued creatures, the volunteers' only recourse was to release them, turn them loose as close as possible to where they found them. They had no room in the boat for more than a few at a time, and figured at least the dogs and cats would know the territory and have a foot up for survival over an unfamiliar environment.

So this particular cat found himself where the rescuers' boat had slowly drifted, between St. Claude and Claiborne avenues in the Lower Ninth Ward, an area which had been particularly ravaged by the failure of the concrete walls of the Industrial Canal. There was only one house undamaged by the flood above the water. They put the cat on the dry front steps and sped off to their next rescue.

"Mowf," he said, tilting his head as they sped away.

He watched for a long time, thinking that they might return and offer him food again. When the sun began to set, he resigned himself to the fact that they would not come back, and began to climb the tall set of steps that led to an elevated front porch. It was a long way up. Which was a good thing, because the house, while tilting a bit with the surge, had stayed well above the water and out of the destructive wake of floating debris. Actually, the house seemed to have only minor damage, though there didn't seem to be humans about.

He began to hope that there might be an abandoned cache of food to be rooted out. That was when he heard the noises. He instantly jumped into alert mode. Other than the rescuers, he had not had many pleasant encounters with the human kind.

First there was a shuffling, then gurgling watery noises, and finally a jumbledy mumbledy sort of human vocalization, followed by the front door slamming open.

There stood a very grey, very fragile-looking human female,

holding a mop and bucket. She spotted him immediately.

"*Eh bien!*" she all but yelled, "*Je serai une vache en patins à roulettes!* I'll be a cow on roller skates, if it ain't another survivor!" she exclaimed loudly. "I sorta figured it was me alone out here. And now here comes a handsome black *chaton,* just lookin' like he wants to hep. Damn fine. Come on in, *mon fils,*" she said, holding open the door. "It don't look like much jes now, what with all the wind an' rain whirlin' about for two days, but I'm almost back. No 'lectricity, but I gots me water and gas, and now I gots me somebody to tawk to. Damn fine. Lemme git you somethin' to et, son."

And she did.

He had never had cornbread soaked in red eye gravy before, could not imagine what it was even as he ate it, but it certainly tasted just fine.

"Thought you might like 'at, son. My pork drippins would make cardboard taste good." She stopped for a moment to muse. "'Son.' Don't sound right. You need a proper name, you do. Hmmm, how's about 'Blackie'? I mean you are mostly black, after all. But, no, that sounds too much like I'd be callin' you 'Darkie.' Ain't proper these days to be makin' such talk. Hmmm."

She mused for a moment, and then her head ticked up. She was smiling. "How's about we just ditch that 'Blackie' business an' make you a gennelman? How's about '*Mister B*'? You'd be a proper *monsieur.* That oughta be awright."

She bent over and petted his head.

"How's about that: Mister B? That name awright wichew?"

"Mowf," said Mister B. He meant it.

"An' me, I'm Mathilde-Marie. Mathilde-Marie LeBlanc. Call me Matty. Glad ta meetcha, B."

The newly-designated cat raised his right paw in recognition of their formal introduction. He also allowed his ears to be rubbed. That truly sealed the deal.

Mister B and Matty began a lasting partnership that day.

He quickly developed a taste for red eye gravy, which led him to prefer it over any commercially canned or bagged items said to nourish cats, no matter how costly.

Likewise she found such a delight in his purring that she could not fall asleep without the B rumbling in place on the pillow next to hers, a pillow she embroidered with his name. Just so he would know he always had a place.

About six months after the departure of the storm and the arrival of the cat, the parish priest returned from exile in Houston and re-opened a church a few blocks west of the Industrial Canal, just in time for the annually scheduled Blessing of the Animals.

The Upper Ninth Ward below St. Claude Avenue was historically home to Creole families, and many of the *gens de couleurs.* These "free people of color" were the descendants of educated, professional Franco-Africans who had migrated to New Orleans and settled into modestly comfortable lives in the city. But since 1900 the Upper 9, also called "Bywater" as it was bordered on the south by the somewhat-water-based Mississippi River, had swung back and forth in the ethnic makeup of new arrivals. Happily presenting multiple identities while moving into the 21st century.

At the moment, however, the recently inundated neighborhood was scarcely populated at all.

It was a long walk across the canal-locks bridge from the Lower Nine, especially since she was carrying a rather weighty and restless cat, but Madame LeBlanc knew it was the right thing to do.

She had early on discovered how much she loved Mr. B, waking in the middle of the night to look at him, and praying: "Please, God, if you really there, give us a bit a time here, huh?"

She needed the church to help protect her new companion, and she was willing to pay the price of foot travel. If she got really tired, she figured that maybe she would put her thumb out to try and catch a ride with some of those nice National Guard boys in their big green trucks.

So she put on her nicest dress, then spent an hour searching the house for her oddly-shaped eyeglasses, so she could see whatever street signs remained in place.

And so she could read the prayer card.

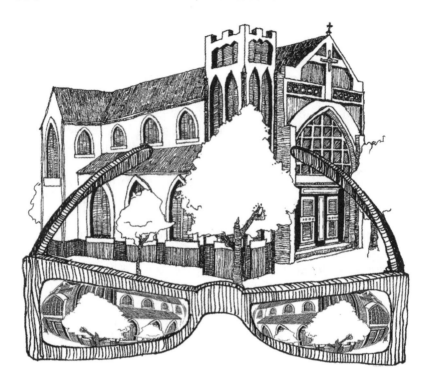

Matty had found the stylish 2.5x magnifying glasses in a somewhat avant-garde drugstore display on Canal Street, some eighteen months earlier. She suspected she already needed a substantial increase in prescription strength, but she liked how the glasses framed her face.

It was indeed a long walk to the church, but Matty and the B arrived in time to get a place at the end of the line for animal blessing. Behind a Rottweiler, a parrot, and two Vietnamese potbellied pigs who each got a brief prayer, some hand-waving and a small dousing with holy water.

Mr. B was none too crazy about having water sprinkled on his face, but if it made Matty feel better, he decided he'd go along.

A strange human male wearing tuxedo-ish black and white clothing stood over him, waved his paw and started mumbling: "*Au nom du père et du fils . . .*" The smoke machine smelled pretty good. Mr. B dozed off during the rest.

At the end of all the hoorah, Matty seemed pleased. Their family arrangement was all settled in her mind now, and on his part Mr. B could feel the bond somehow cemented. They managed to catch a ride all the way back home in a truck driven by an elderly tomato farmer, a gent who seemed mightily taken with Madame LeBlanc, and who offered her his phone number.

"Ain't got no phone," she told him. "Just come visit whenever you feel like it."

Seemed a good enough prospect for the farmer, who waved happily as he drove off. And that was that.

Sure enough, at the end of the day Mr. B had indeed got himself blessed, even though he had no idea what "blessed" was. Other than wet.

Historically, he was none too fond of wet.

So, a once-feral tuxedo with a snipped right ear came to happily cohabit an ever-so-slightly tilted house in the Lower Ninth Ward with an aging human named Mathilde-Marie LeBlanc.

And both became happier.

As Matty's *grand-mère* always told her: *"Il ne faut pas grand-chose pour être heureux quand on a déjà bon coeur."*

She was right. It doesn't take much to be happy when you already have a good heart.

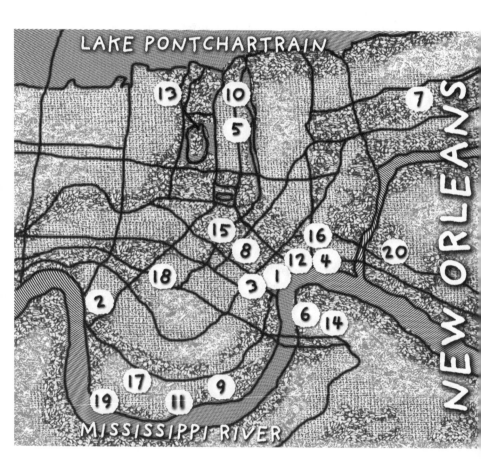